CIA Agent  er
AKA The Huntress

Dedication

For those who dare to embrace the darkness within, and for those who seek redemption in the shadows. May you find solace in the knowledge that even the most twisted soul can yearn for a flicker of light.

Preface

This is not a story for the faint of heart. It delves into the darkest recesses of the human psyche, where morality is a tattered flag and justice is a twisted reflection of what we hold dear. Elsa Gardner is not your typical heroine. She is a predator who walks the tightrope between control and chaos, a woman who embraces her darkness and wields it as a weapon. Prepare to be challenged, to question your own perceptions of right and wrong. Prepare to meet the darkness within, and perhaps, find a flicker of understanding.

Introduction

Some are born into darkness, their hearts echoing with a primal yearning for violence. Elsa Gardner is one such soul. From the innocent killing of a goose in her childhood to the calculated execution of a college classmate, she has always danced with the seductive allure of her own destructive impulses. Driven by a hunger for power and a twisted sense of justice, Elsa will become a weapon against the very darkness that resides within her. But can she truly be a force for good when her own heart beats to the rhythm of destruction?

The Echo of Childhood

The world was a tapestry of muted greens and browns, the air heavy with the scent of damp earth and the quiet hum of insects. Seven-year-old Elsa, a wisp of a girl with eyes the color of storm clouds, knelt by the side of the pond, her gaze fixed on the graceful white goose that glided across the water. It was a creature of beauty, its feathers shimmering like polished silver in the afternoon sun. But Elsa saw
something else – a vulnerability, a fragile life that could be extinguished with a simple flick of a wrist.

She had been captivated by death since she was a toddler, drawn to the macabre with a morbid curiosity that chilled her parents to the bone. Her fascination started with a dead sparrow, its tiny body lying lifeless in the garden, its once vibrant feathers now dull and matted. She spent hours studying it, marveling at the stillness, the finality of it all.

Her fascination turned to obsession. She would follow her grandmother to the local cemetery, fascinated by the rows of headstones, each marking a life extinguished. She'd trace the etched letters, whispering the names of the dead as if they were incantations, a whispered communion with the departed.

Her parents, concerned and confused,
tried to curb her
morbid curiosity. They tried to fill her
world with the vibrant colors of life –
with blooming flowers and playful
puppies –but Elsa remained drawn
to the darkness, to the finality of
death.

On that day by the pond, the
goose, with its graceful
movements and its serene gaze,
held a different kind of

appeal. It was a living creature, a
symbol of life, and its existence was a

testament to the cycle of birth and death. But it also represented something more – a fragile life, a fleeting moment in time that could be erased with a single act.

Elsa knew that what she was about to do was wrong. It was a transgression against life itself, a betrayal of the innocence that still clung to her. But the dark allure of death, the intoxicating power it held, was too strong to resist.

She reached into her pocket, her hand closing around the smooth, cold surface of the rock she had collected earlier. The goose, unaware of its impending doom, continued its graceful journey across the water. Elsa, her heart pounding with a mixture of fear and anticipation, watched its every movement.

She raised her arm, the rock heavy in her hand, and the goose, in its moment of blissful unawareness, became the object of her morbid fascination. The rock, propelled by the force of her will, arced through the air, a deadly missile aimed at the unsuspecting bird.

Time seemed to slow down, the world fading into a blur of colors and sounds. The goose, sensing its imminent danger, lifted its head, its eyes widening in fear, but it was too late.
The rock struck its head with a sickening thud, the sound

reverberating through the tranquil stillness of the afternoon.

The goose crumpled, its graceful form collapsing onto the surface of the water, creating a cascade of ripples that spread outwards, reflecting the darkness that now resided within Elsa's soul.

The act was done. The goose, its life extinguished, lay motionless on the water, its serene gaze now forever frozen in a mask of death. Elsa, her hand trembling slightly, stood there, staring down at her handiwork. The guilt, the fear, the

strange sense of accomplishment – they all mingled within her,

creating a confusing cocktail of
emotions that left her both
exhilarated and terrified.

She had taken a life, a tiny flicker of
life, and the act had left an indelible
mark on her soul. It was the first step
on a path that would lead her to the
darkest corners of her own mind, a
path that would ultimately define her
life, a path of
destruction that she had set in motion
with a simple flick of the wrist.

The Seed of Violence

The air hung heavy with the cloying scent of honeysuckle and damp earth, the humid summer air thick with the promise of an impending storm. Ten-year-old Elsa, perched precariously on the rickety fence, felt the tension in her small frame. She knew the storm wasn't just brewing in the sky; it was gathering inside her too, a tempest of rage and fear churning beneath the surface of her childish facade.

Her eyes, reflecting the gathering darkness, were fixated on the lone figure in the distance, his silhouette stark against the fading light. Her father. He was coming home, and with him, the oppressive weight of his silence, the chilling shadow of his anger. It was an anger that often manifested in the form of her mother's screams, the shattering of glass, the guttural rasp of his voice as he roared at the world.

Elsa's world was a symphony of chaos, punctuated by the discordant notes of his violence. He was a storm cloud, a constant threat hovering above their lives, a dark specter she learned to live with, to anticipate, to fear.

The sound of a car door slamming shattered the silence, sending a jolt of adrenaline through her. He was close. She watched as his hulking form lumbered out of the car, the familiar scent of stale beer and sweat preceding him like a harbinger of doom.

She knew the routine. He'd come inside, the anger simmering beneath his rough exterior, waiting to erupt. Her mother, a fragile bird trapped in a cage, would cower, her voice a barely audible whisper. She'd try to appease him, a futile attempt to calm the storm within him.

The memories, vivid and sharp, replayed in Elsa's mind, each scene a cruel tableau of her childhood. The sound of her mother's cries, the thud of fists against flesh, the cold, hollow fear that permeated their home.

That night, the anger had been particularly intense, a whirlwind of rage unleashed upon her mother. Elsa, huddled in the corner, watched as her father, a monster in the guise of a man, rained blows upon her mother's slender frame.

She had been a witness to the world's cruelty, a helpless observer of the darkness that consumed her father. It had ignited something inside her, a smoldering ember of rage, a burning desire for retribution.

The sound of her father's voice, a guttural growl that resonated through the walls, pulled her back to the present. She knew he was inside, his anger simmering, waiting for the smallest spark to ignite it.

It was then, in that moment of fear and rage, that the seed of violence was planted within her. She looked out at the geese huddled in the nearby pond, their serene presence a stark contrast to the storm brewing within her. It was as if they embodied a world she longed for, a world untouched by the darkness that consumed her.

But even they, she realized, were not immune to the cruelty of nature, the harsh reality of the world. Her father had often taken her hunting, taught her to handle a gun, to hunt with precision and ruthlessness. He'd instilled in her a respect for the power of death, the beauty and the horror of it all.

And as she watched the geese, a strange sensation coursed through her. A feeling of power, of control. She saw the way they waddled, oblivious to their own vulnerability, their

feathered necks outstretched in a display of innocent trust. It was this vulnerability that sparked a chilling thought, a terrifyingly alluring idea.

The storm was gathering within her, a storm of vengeance and a dark, twisted sense of justice. She knew she had to act, to make them understand, to show them the truth of the world.

With a newfound sense of purpose, Elsa reached for the heavy stone she'd collected from the field. She felt the cold, smooth surface, the weight of it in her hand. It was the instrument of her justice, her twisted way of making the world right.

She took a step closer to the pond, her gaze fixed on the geese, their serene presence now seeming mockingly
innocent. She raised her hand, the stone glistening in the fading light, and unleashed the storm that had been brewing within her.

The geese, once peaceful and oblivious, now squawked in terror, their wings beating frantically against the air as they tried to escape the cruel reality that had befallen them.

The stone found its target, the impact a sickening thud that echoed across the pond. A goose, its neck twisted at an unnatural angle, fell limply to the water. Its life, once vibrant and full, extinguished in a cruel and brutal display of power.

Elsa stood there, bathed in the fading light, her small frame trembling with a strange mix of terror and exhilaration. She had tasted blood, felt the thrill of the hunt, the intoxicating power of death.

The seed of violence had sprouted, its roots twisting deep within her soul. It was a darkness she had inherited, a legacy

passed down from a father who had taught her to embrace the darkness, to wield it as a weapon.

The storm had passed, but the echo of its fury lingered, a chilling reminder of the violence that lay dormant within her, waiting to be unleashed.

She knew it was only a matter of time before the storm

returned, before her desire for retribution would consume her once more. She was a seed of violence, a hurricane waiting to be born. And she was just getting started.

The College Years

The college years were a carefully constructed stage for Elsa, a facade of normalcy hiding the chilling truth she carried within. She blended in with the throngs of students, attending classes, joining clubs, and navigating the social landscape with an almost unnerving ease. Elsa embraced the

anonymity of the campus, a haven where she could
disappear amongst the masses, carefully crafting her persona as an ordinary, albeit slightly introverted, young woman. She was a master of disguise, a chameleon who could shift her colors to blend in with her surroundings. Her apartment was a testament to her calculated life, each object chosen for its purpose. The walls were adorned with meticulously framed art prints, each depicting scenes of nature's serenity, a carefully curated facade meant to mask the storm raging within.

Elsa's seemingly ordinary life was a carefully curated
illusion, a carefully constructed mask. The truth, however, lay buried

beneath the surface, lurking beneath the veneer of normalcy. While her days were filled with the mundane rhythms of college life, her nights were consumed by a

different reality, a dark underworld where she nurtured the sinister impulses that resided within. Her bedroom, a

sanctuary for her nocturnal activities, was a tableau of the darkness she embraced. Instead of textbooks, she indulged in the grim literature of true crime, dissecting the minds of notorious serial killers, gleaning insights into their twisted motivations. Each gruesome detail, each chilling confession, fueled the flames of her own insatiable curiosity.

Elsa's obsession with crime and her fascination with the macabre were not just a morbid curiosity but a deep-seated

need to understand the darkness that pulsed within her own soul. She was a predator in sheep's clothing, a predator who could easily blend in with the flock, but whose predatory instincts were always on the prowl. Her chosen major, criminal justice and forensics, was a gateway to the world she craved, a way to delve into the intricacies of human behavior, particularly the dark, twisted corners of the human psyche. She excelled in her studies, devouring information like a starving beast. She saw it as a kind of intellectual feast, a way to understand the very mechanisms that drove her own destructive desires. She spent hours in the campus library, poring over textbooks on criminal psychology, forensic science, and behavioral analysis, her mind constantly absorbing knowledge that was both fascinating and terrifying.

Elsa's physical prowess was another facet of her carefully crafted persona. She had a lean, muscular build, honed through years of intensive MMA training. She was a force to be reckoned with, capable of inflicting serious damage, a fact that was both exhilarating and unsettling. Her training wasn't just about physical strength, though. It was about control, about mastering the power within her, a power that she knew could easily slip out of control, a power that could consume her. Elsa's training was a balancing act, a constant battle against the darkness that threatened to engulf her. She pushed her limits, testing her endurance, all the while knowing that her own internal demons lurked just beneath the surface, waiting for the right moment to erupt.

The façade she presented was a carefully crafted illusion, a shield against the harsh realities of her inner world. She was a master of deception, a chameleon who could effortlessly blend in with her surroundings, but her true nature was a secret hidden beneath the surface, a secret that she knew could shatter her carefully constructed world at any moment. Beneath the veneer of normalcy, Elsa was a predator, a wolf

in sheep's clothing, meticulously controlling her impulses, but always aware that the darkness within her could consume her.

The campus, a place of youthful exuberance and academic aspirations, was a hunting ground for her. Her sharp eyes, always observing, scanning for signs of vulnerability, for potential prey. She had an uncanny ability to sense weakness, to spot those who were unguarded, those who had let their walls down, those who were ripe for the picking.

Elsa's gaze was like a predator's, unblinking, calculating, seeking out the weakest link in the chain, the most
vulnerable target. Her classmates were nothing more than subjects to her, an endless stream of potential targets for her dark impulses.

Her days were a carefully curated performance, a series of calculated steps designed to maintain her facade of
normalcy. But when the sun dipped below the horizon, and the shadows stretched across the campus, Elsa transformed. The predator within her awakened, her instincts sharpened, her senses heightened. She was a creature

of the night, a creature of darkness, and the world around her became a playground for her twisted desires. Each kill, each act of violence, was a carefully orchestrated performance, a meticulous dance of death where she was both the choreographer and the star. The adrenaline rush, the thrill of the chase, the sense of power and control, all fueled her desire to continue down this path. She was a monster, but a monster who thrived on the very act of killing. There was a perverse sense of beauty in the chaos, a disturbing aesthetic in the violence that she unleashed. And the world around her, oblivious to the darkness that she carried within, continued to be her stage, her canvas, her hunting ground. She was a phantom, a ghost in the machine, a creature of darkness who thrived in the shadows, and her reign of terror was only just beginning.

The shadows were her sanctuary, the darkness her element. And in the heart of the seemingly innocent college campus, she walked a tightrope between her carefully crafted façade and the terrifying reality of her own nature. The darkness within her whispered, urged her to succumb, to embrace the monster she was destined to become. But Elsa, for now, held on to the facade, the carefully curated image of normalcy.

But deep down, she knew that her true nature was just

beneath the surface, waiting to
be unleashed.

The First Kill

The air hung heavy with the scent of
damp earth and the metallic tang of
blood. Elsa, barely a woman yet,
stood in the clearing, the lifeless
goose sprawled at her feet, its once-
proud wings now limp and stained
crimson. The moonlight, filtered
through the skeletal branches of the
ancient oak, painted grotesque
shadows across the scene, a stark
reminder of the act she had just

committed.

It had been a calculated execution,
swift and precise, a
chilling echo of the darkness that
lurked within her. The goose, a sleek
white bird with eyes as black as
midnight, had been her target, an
innocent pawn in a game she hadn't
fully understood. But she had felt the
thrill of the kill, a primal rush of
power that sent a shiver of excitement
down her spine.

Elsa knelt beside the dead bird,
her fingers tracing the outline of
its feathered body. There was a
fascination, a morbid curiosity in
her touch, a desire to understand
the mechanics of life and death
that went far beyond the innocent

curiosity of a child. Her gaze
lingered on the goose's lifeless
eyes, their once-bright gleam
now
extinguished, a stark reflection of
the emptiness she felt within.

A whisper of wind rustled through the
leaves, carrying with it the faint scent
of decaying leaves and the memory of
her grandfather's gruff voice, his
warning echoing in her mind: "That
darkness you carry, Elsa, it's a hunger.
And it will only grow stronger with
time."

She had been a child then, oblivious to the
meaning behind

his words. But the goose, its lifeless form a silent testament to her actions, had awakened a new awareness within her. The darkness, a silent passenger in the depths of her soul, had finally begun to stir.

Elsa's childhood, though seemingly idyllic on the surface, was shrouded in an unsettling undercurrent of fear. Her parents, both deeply religious, had instilled in her a sense of moral responsibility, a strict adherence to their beliefs. Yet, she felt an undeniable disconnect, a longing for something darker, a hunger for something that went against the grain of their expectations.

The whispers of her grandfather's warnings, though

dismissed as the ramblings of an old man, resonated in her subconscious, a cryptic message from a forgotten past. He had been a man of contradictions, a devout believer yet possessing an unnerving fascination with the macabre. He would regale her with tales of haunted forests and vengeful spirits, his voice dropping to a hushed whisper as he described the gruesome details of historical atrocities.

Elsa, captivated by his stories, felt a strange pull towards the darkness, an irresistible force that beckoned her towards the shadows. It was during one of her grandfather's tales, a chilling account of a woman who had been accused of witchcraft and burned at the stake, that the first seed of violence had been planted.

Her grandfather, his eyes glittering with an unnatural light, had described the woman's execution with a chilling detail.
He spoke of the flames consuming her body, the screams piercing the night, the scent of burning flesh lingering in the air long after the pyre had died down. The image of the woman, consumed by the flames, was seared into Elsa's memory, a haunting reminder of the power and the brutality of human nature.

As she listened to his story, a strange sensation crept into her, a feeling of both revulsion and fascination. The brutality of the act, the raw power of the flames, the woman's screams echoing in her mind, ignited a spark within her, a flicker of something dark and primal. It was a sensation she couldn't define, a feeling she both embraced and feared.

Her grandfather's death, sudden and unexpected, left a
gaping hole in her life. The stories, the whispers, the
unsettling fascination with the dark side of humanity, they all vanished with him, leaving behind a void that only
intensified with time. The seed of violence, sown in her childhood,

continued to grow, nurtured by the darkness that resided within her, a darkness that she was beginning to understand.

The goose, its lifeless form a chilling reminder of her actions, became a turning point, a symbol of the power she held within her. The darkness, once a distant whisper, had now become a tangible entity, a predator that lurked within her, demanding to be unleashed.

The years passed, blurring into a hazy montage of normalcy.
Elsa excelled in her studies, a promising student with a bright future. She embraced the façade of a happy, well-adjusted young woman, meticulously crafting a life

that fit the expectations of her family and society. Yet, beneath the surface, a darkness simmered, a hidden truth she guarded with an unwavering resolve.

It was in college, surrounded by a sea of faces, that she began to understand the true nature of her darkness. The camaraderie, the shared laughter, the sense of belonging, it all felt hollow, a charade that did little to alleviate the emptiness she carried within. The world she inhabited, a world of normalcy and conformity, felt suffocating, a cage that stifled the predator within.

Elsa, drawn to the shadows, found solace in the anonymity of the night. She would wander through the deserted streets, the city lights casting long, distorted shadows that danced in the darkness. In the solitude of those nights, she would find herself, a reflection of the darkness that resided within her.

It was during one of these solitary walks that she encountered him, a man who embodied the darkness she so desperately sought to escape. He was a predator, a master manipulator, his eyes holding a chilling gleam that sent a shiver down her spine. He saw her, not for who she was but for what she could be, a kindred spirit, a soul lost in the labyrinth of darkness.

He introduced her to a world of secrets, a world where the lines between right and wrong were blurred, where the darkness held a seductive allure. He offered her a taste of the power that resided within her, a glimpse into the abyss she had so desperately tried to ignore.

It was a dangerous game, a dance with the devil, but Elsa, drawn to the thrill, played along. She reveled in the power she felt, the sense of control she held over others, the intoxicating sensation of walking on the edge. The darkness, once a lurking shadow, now felt like a part of her, an inseparable part of her being.

And then, one night, it happened. The act, calculated and precise, an execution as cold and calculating as a chess player making his final move. The college classmate, a charming young man with a disarming smile, had become her target. He had wronged her, a minor transgression, an act of carelessness that had set off a chain reaction within her.

It started with a feeling, a deep-seated resentment that

festered in the depths of her soul. He had been reckless, careless, a predator in his own right, leaving a trail of broken hearts and shattered dreams in his wake. The injustice, however insignificant in the grand scheme of things, was a catalyst, a trigger that ignited the darkness within her.

She had planned it meticulously, a dance of shadows, a game of manipulation. She had lured him into a trap, a calculated act of revenge designed to inflict upon him the same pain he had inflicted on others. The execution was swift and silent, a dark symphony played out in the silence of the night.

The thrill of the kill, a rush of adrenaline, a sensation that sent a shiver down her spine, it was exhilarating,

intoxicating. Yet, as the dust settled, as the adrenaline faded, a chilling realization washed over her. The darkness she had embraced, it was a dangerous mistress, demanding her complete surrender.

The goose, a faint memory now, was a distant echo of the darkness that had consumed her. The first kill, a chilling harbinger of things to come, had set her on a path she could not escape, a descent into darkness that would forever shape her destiny.

The Aftermath

The crisp autumn air carried the scent of decaying leaves and a strange, metallic tang that clung to Elsa's senses. She stood in the shadows of the college library, the weight of her actions pressing down on her like a physical burden. The echo of the gunshots, the sickening crunch of bone, the terrified scream – all were etched into her memory, a haunting soundtrack playing on a loop in her mind.

The college classmate, a boy named Mark, had been a petty bully, a source of constant irritation. But Elsa had never imagined she would kill him. It had been a calculated act, a response to his callous cruelty, his arrogant disregard for her. Yet, in the aftermath, she felt a peculiar mix of exhilaration and dread, a potent cocktail that left her reeling.

The exhilaration was a dangerous, seductive whisper, a dark echo of the power she felt surging through her veins in that moment. The world seemed to shrink, to become a stage for her performance, a testament to her control. The dread, however, was a persistent chill that settled in her gut, a constant reminder of the irreversible act she had committed. It was a gnawing fear, a dark premonition that she might be losing her grip, slipping deeper into the abyss she had always feared.

As she walked back to her dorm room, her steps were lighter, her gait almost buoyant. The crisp air tasted different, charged with the electric thrill of her actions. But the shadow of her guilt lingered, a cold hand on her shoulder, whispering warnings she couldn't ignore. She could smell the blood on her clothes, a persistent reminder of the violence she had unleashed.

In the quiet of her room, she stripped off the clothes she wore during the deed, the act of shedding them a symbolic act of purging her conscience. But even the shower, the torrent of water washing over her, couldn't wash away the stain of her actions. Her reflection in the mirror was

distorted, her eyes dark pools reflecting the torment within.

The room, once a sanctuary, now felt like a prison. The walls seemed to close in, suffocating her with the weight of her secret. The silence was deafening, broken only by the rhythmic beat of her racing heart. She tried to convince herself that what she had done was justified, that Mark had deserved his fate. But the rationalizations felt hollow, the words failing to convince the part of her that knew she had crossed a line.

Days turned into weeks, each one a struggle against the mounting guilt and the growing fear. She tried to maintain her normalcy, her carefully constructed facade, but it was becoming increasingly difficult. The paranoia crept in, whispers of suspicion and apprehension echoing in the hallways. Her hands shook, her movements were jerky, her senses hyper-sensitive. The weight of her secret was a crushing burden, threatening to suffocate her.

One evening, she found herself staring out her window, the cityscape spread out before her like a canvas of glittering lights and distant sounds. It was a scene of vibrant life, yet it felt alien, a stark contrast to the darkness that had seeped into her soul.

The world seemed to have shifted on its axis, the colors muted, the sounds muffled. The sense of isolation was palpable, the chasm between her and everyone else growing wider with each passing day. She felt like a ghost, existing on the periphery of the world, trapped in a cage of her own

making.

A single tear rolled down her cheek, hot against her skin. It was a tear of sorrow, of guilt, of a soul grappling with the consequences of its actions.

She couldn't explain it, couldn't
rationalize it, only felt the deep pang
of regret, the gnawing realization
that her life had irrevocably changed.

Her first kill, a calculated act of
revenge, had awakened something
within her, a darkness that she had
always feared. It was a dangerous
power, a seductive allure that
whispered promises of control and
justice, but it was also a beast she
couldn't control, a fire that threatened
to consume her.

The goose she had killed as a child,
a senseless act of cruelty, had been
a chilling foreshadowing of the
darkness that resided within her.
But it had been a fleeting, childlike
act, a spark that hadn't yet ignited.

Mark, however, was a different story. He was a turning point, a catalyst that had unleashed a torrent of violence that she couldn't contain.

The guilt was a constant companion, a relentless reminder of her transgression. It was a sharp pain, a constant ache in the pit of her stomach, a dark cloud that shadowed her every thought. It was a feeling she could never outrun, a truth she couldn't escape.

The thought of her actions, of the blood staining her hands, haunted her dreams. She saw Mark's face in the darkness, his eyes wide with terror, his voice screaming for mercy. She heard the gunshots echoing in her

ears, the echoes
reverberating through her very being.
She couldn't shake the image of his
lifeless body, the blood pooling
around him like a crimson halo.

She felt the weight of her secret
bearing down on her, a physical
burden that she could no longer
ignore. The world,

once full of possibilities, now felt
constricted, the boundaries of her life
shrinking to the confines of her room,
the walls closing in on her.

But even in the depths of her despair,
there was a flicker of something else,

a spark of a different kind. It was a yearning, a desperate craving for something more, a way to escape the darkness that had enveloped her. It was a faint glimmer of hope, a whisper of redemption that resonated within her tormented soul.

The Violation

The apartment door slammed shut behind Elsa, the sound echoing through the sterile hallway. It was a sound she knew all too well, a sound that always carried the weight of her roommate, Lily's, laughter. But tonight, the laughter was absent, replaced by a chilling silence that felt thick enough to choke.

Elsa's stomach churned with an unfamiliar sensation, a blend of nausea and a primal rage that tightened her jaw and sent a tremor through her body. It wasn't just the silence that was wrong, it was the way Lily's belongings lay strewn across the floor, their usual order replaced by a chaotic mess. A wave of icy fear washed over her, a premonition that something was terribly wrong.

Elsa's fingers, normally so quick and agile, fumbled with the key, her heart pounding a frantic rhythm against her ribs. She pushed the door open, the scent of stale alcohol and something else, something metallic and acrid, hitting her like a physical blow. The air felt thick, laden with a palpable tension that sent shivers down her spine.

Lily lay on the floor, her once vibrant auburn hair matted with blood, her body twisted at an unnatural angle. The sight of her, broken and vulnerable, ignited a volcanic eruption of fury within Elsa. It wasn't just the blood staining the carpet, it was the look of terror frozen on her face, the way her eyes, usually sparkling with life, were now vacant and unseeing.

The realization of what had happened, the brutal reality of the situation, crashed down on Elsa with the force of a tidal wave. Lily, her friend, her confidante, had been violated, her

body desecrated by the hands of a predator. A guttural growl escaped Elsa's throat, the sound of a wild animal cornered and enraged.

Her mind, always a battlefield between chaos and control, now teetered on the precipice of madness. Elsa's training, the years of rigorous MMA training, kicked in, a familiar sense of purpose taking hold as the primal rage coursed through her veins.

Her eyes, normally a cool gray, now burned with a cold fury. The air around her crackled with an unsettling energy, the scent of blood mingling with the sharp tang of adrenaline. This wasn't just a violation of her roommate, it was a violation of her own sense of order, a transgression that would not go unanswered.

She knelt beside Lily, her hands trembling with the raw force of her emotions. She could feel the faint pulse of her heart, weak but still alive, a fragile ember of hope amidst the ashes of despair. Elsa closed her eyes, breathing in the metallic scent of blood, the air thick with the phantom presence of the attacker.

The rage, a consuming fire, fueled her desire for retribution. The hunt, the meticulous pursuit of the perpetrator, became her sole focus, a singular purpose that consumed her every thought, every instinct. She was no longer just Elsa Gardner, the woman who lived a quiet life in the shadows. She was a predator, a hunter, and she would not rest until the one who had violated Lily paid the ultimate price.

Elsa's fingers traced the outline of Lily's face, the touch a silent promise. "I'll make them pay," she whispered, the words laced with a chilling determination. She stood, her body a coiled spring of restrained energy, the darkness within her a palpable force. The apartment, a witness to the

unspeakable act, now
echoed with the whispers
of vengeance.

The hunt had begun. It was a hunt
fueled by rage, driven by a thirst for
justice, and Elsa, consumed by a
primal hunger for revenge, would not
rest until the predator was brought to
heel.

A Twisted Hunt

The violation of her roommate, the
brutal intrusion into her sanctuary,
ignited a firestorm within Elsa. It

wasn't just rage, though that burned bright and fierce. It was a primal hunger for retribution, a thirst for justice that resonated deep within her soul. The seed of violence, planted in her childhood, had blossomed into a poisonous vine, wrapping around her heart and squeezing out any semblance of compassion.

Her roommate, Sarah, was a wisp of a girl, a fragile butterfly in the storm of Elsa's world. Yet, Elsa felt a fierce loyalty to her, a protective instinct that she hadn't realized she possessed. Sarah was a source of light in her darkness, a reminder that even in the abyss, there was a sliver of hope.

Now, that hope was shattered, replaced by a burning,

consuming desire for
vengeance.

Elsa delved into the investigation, her
mind a labyrinth of logic and
deduction. She meticulously pieced
together
fragments of information, her keen
forensic eye noticing details that
others overlooked. Every clue, every
whisper, was a step closer to the
monster who had dared to violate her
sanctuary.

The hunt became an obsession, a
relentless pursuit that consumed her
every waking moment. She stalked
the
shadows, a predator seeking its prey.
The fear that had once been her
weakness now became her weapon, a

chilling presence that sent a shiver down the spines of those who crossed her path.

The perpetrator, a shadowy figure lurking in the underbelly of the city, was a master of deception. He moved through the

night with the stealth of a phantom, leaving no trace, no witness. But Elsa was relentless, driven by a hunger that could not be satiated.

She traced his movements, piecing together the fragmented puzzle of his crimes. Every night, she followed him, her senses sharpened, her instincts honed. She knew that the monster was not merely a criminal; he was a predator, a deviant who reveled in the fear and pain he inflicted.

Elsa wasn't content with merely catching him; she wanted to break him, to make him pay for the violation he had committed. She wanted to see the terror in his eyes, to feel the fear that he had inflicted on others. Her desire for revenge was no longer a dark impulse; it had become an all-consuming obsession, a fire that burned with a dangerous intensity.

The opportunity presented itself on a night like any other, shrouded in the inky darkness that enveloped the city. The scent of desperation hung heavy in the air, a tangible presence that Elsa could almost taste. She found him, the predator, in a secluded alleyway, a place he had chosen for his twisted acts.

Elsa had crafted her plan with precision, a symphony of pain and retribution. She lured him with a carefully crafted trap, playing on his vulnerabilities, exploiting his darkest desires.

The alleyway became a stage for a twisted dance of vengeance, a macabre performance where the lines between hunter and hunted blurred into an indistinguishable mess.

As the monster fell, Elsa felt a rush of adrenaline, a primal satisfaction that coursed through her veins. It wasn't simply a victory over evil; it was a validation of her own darkness, a confirmation that she was a force to be reckoned with. But even as the adrenaline subsided, a chilling realization

dawned upon her.

The monster was dead, but the darkness that had driven him lived on. And within her, that darkness stirred, a restless beast yearning to be unleashed. In that moment, Elsa understood that she had crossed a threshold, a point of no return. She had become the very thing she had set out to destroy, a predator consumed by her own twisted desires.

The police arrived, sirens blaring, their flashing lights illuminating the scene of her crime. As the officers surrounded her, a wave of calm washed over Elsa. She knew this was the end of one chapter, but the story was far from over. She was caught red-handed, her world shattered by the undeniable truth of her actions.

The officers' faces were etched with suspicion and disgust. They saw the monster, but they didn't see the woman, the victim of a childhood she could never escape. They didn't understand the darkness that consumed her, the insatiable hunger for retribution that had driven her to this point.

She was led away, the weight of her actions pressing down on her like a physical burden. In the sterile confines of the interrogation room, she faced the consequences of her choices. The world she had carefully constructed, a world where she could control her darkness, had crumbled.

But as the officers grilled her, a glimmer of hope emerged. An agent, a man with eyes that held a hidden depth, offered her a chilling ultimatum: join the CIA, become a weapon against the very darkness that resided within her, or face a lifetime behind bars.

The choice was stark, a precipice between redemption and damnation. Elsa, driven by a hunger for power and a twisted sense of justice, chose the former. She embraced her

darkness, transforming it into a weapon, a tool for her own twisted version of justice.

As she stepped into the shadows of the CIA, Elsa knew that her life would never be the same. She had become a hunter, a predator unleashed, and the world would never know the darkness that lurked beneath her meticulously crafted facade. But in that darkness, she found a strange sense of purpose, a twisted sense of belonging.

The path ahead was treacherous, a journey into the heart of darkness. She would face monsters, both inside and out, and the lines between right and wrong would blur into an indistinguishable mess. But Elsa was ready, a weapon forged in the fires of her own tormented past.

She was Elsa Gardner, and she was the hunter.

The Lure

The acrid scent of bleach and fear
clung to the air, a
suffocating blanket draped over the
small apartment. The walls, once
adorned with vibrant posters and
whimsical trinkets, were now stark
white, scrubbed clean of any trace of
the assault that had violated their
space. Elsa stood in the center of the
sterile room, a figure of controlled
fury, her gaze fixed on the chipped
paint on the bathroom door.

A wave of nausea washed over her,
the memory of her
roommate's trembling voice, her tear-
streaked face, a
visceral reminder of the violation that

had occurred. It wasn't just the physical intrusion, the violation of her friend's body, it was the chilling realization that this kind of darkness could exist in their seemingly safe haven.

Elsa, ever the strategist, had already pieced together the puzzle. She'd meticulously analyzed the forensic evidence, the subtle inconsistencies in the police report, the trail of discarded cigarette butts, the lingering aroma of cheap cologne – each detail a thread woven into the tapestry of the perpetrator's identity. Her mind, a deadly engine fueled by a dark, relentless sense of justice, had already begun to spin, crafting the intricate web of her retribution.

She wasn't a woman who believed in the sanctity of the law, not anymore. The justice system, with its procedural loopholes and bureaucratic red tape, felt like a joke, a cruel parody of justice. For Elsa, justice had a singular, stark definition – an eye for an eye, a life for a life. It was a code etched onto her very soul, born from the twisted embers of her childhood, nurtured by the trauma that had shaped her into the woman she was.

The perpetrator was a shadow, a predator who thrived in the darkness of anonymity. His name was Mark, a drifter with a history of violence, a man who relished the thrill of inflicting pain. Elsa had discovered his past, a twisted trail of broken lives and unsolved assaults, a hidden world where fear and manipulation became tools of dominance.

Her initial investigation, fueled by righteous anger, had quickly morphed into an obsessive hunt. Each piece of information she unearthed, each clue she deciphered, fueled the insatiable fire within her. She'd mapped his movements, charted his routine, a meticulously crafted choreography of revenge. The apartment, now a sterile canvas, was her stage, the city her hunting ground.

The trap was set, a deadly game of cat and mouse, with Elsa as the hunter

and Mark as the hapless prey. She had learned the art of manipulation, her charm a lethal weapon. She'd sent an anonymous message, a siren song of desire, a
carefully crafted invitation that would draw Mark into the web she'd spun.

Mark, as expected, fell into her trap. His desperation was evident in his hurried movements, his nervous glances, the way his fingers trembled as he lit a cigarette. He was a man used to anonymity, a shadow in the dimly lit alleyways, but Elsa had brought him out into the open, exposed him to the stark light of his own culpability.

She led him to the abandoned warehouse, a concrete

labyrinth steeped in the stench of decay and neglect. It was a place where shadows danced and whispers echoed, a fitting stage for the final act of her play. The warehouse was a canvas of her design, a symphony of despair, a chilling monument to her twisted sense of justice.

His fear, palpable in the tense silence, was a symphony to her ears. It was the taste of her own victory, the bitter sweetness of vengeance. He saw the glint of steel in her eyes, the cold, calculated gaze of a predator who had finally cornered her prey. She knew he understood; he knew he was trapped in the web she'd woven.

The fight, brief and brutal, was a
dance of violence, a clash of primal
instincts. Mark, a broken man fueled
by
desperation, met Elsa's fierce
precision with a frenzy of animalistic
rage. The warehouse, a desolate
witness, echoed with the thud of fists
meeting flesh, the chilling scrape of
metal against bone.

He was no match for her. Elsa, with
years of MMA training, was a force of
nature, a whirlwind of destruction.
Each blow, precise and calculated,
was fueled by the righteous fire of her
vengeance. His pleas for mercy were
lost in the chaotic symphony of his

demise.

The warehouse, a stage bathed in the crimson hues of spilled blood, became the final testament to her twisted justice. Elsa, her hands slick with his blood, stood amidst the carnage, her gaze fixed on the crumpled form of her enemy. She had delivered her sentence, enacted her own brand of justice, leaving the world a little less tainted by his darkness.

But victory, in this case, was a hollow victory. The echo of violence resonated through her, a stark reminder of the depths of her own darkness. The chilling truth of her actions, the undeniable reality of her own monstrosity, seeped into her soul like a poison. It was a moment of clarity, a brief glimpse into the abyss she had created, a stark reminder of the price she was paying for her twisted sense of justice.

Elsa, a woman who walked the razor-thin line between predator and protector, had crossed a threshold. She had

become the very monster she was fighting, a chilling reflection of the darkness she sought to eradicate. The world she had chosen, the twisted path she had embraced, was a cruel labyrinth with no exit. The echoes of her actions, a haunting symphony of violence,

would forever be etched onto her soul,
a constant reminder of the price she
paid for her thirst for justice.

The Revelation

The air hung thick with the smell of
bleach and fear. Elsa stood frozen,
her hands shaking as she stared at
the blood-soaked sheets crumpled
at her feet. It was undeniable now.
She was caught, her carefully
constructed facade of
normalcy shattered by the stark reality
of her actions. Her heart hammered
against her ribs, a frantic drumbeat

echoing the chaos within her. She had crossed the line, and there was no turning back.

The apartment felt like a prison cell, its walls closing in on her. She could feel every eye in the building burning into her, judging her, condemning her. The police swarmed the apartment like vultures, their faces emotionless, their gazes cold and calculating.

"You're under arrest," a gruff voice boomed, shattering the suffocating silence. "You have the right to remain silent..." The words were a mantra, a chorus of her impending doom.

Elsa stood there, her body a conduit of fear and defiance. Her mind raced, a whirlwind of thoughts and justifications. She had done what she had to do. He deserved it. He had violated her friend, her family, her sense of justice.

"I'm innocent," she whispered, the words tasting like ash on her tongue. Her voice trembled, but she held her head high, her gaze meeting the cold stare of the officer.

The hours blurred together, a dizzying vortex of interrogation and accusations. The officers pressed her, their questions piercing her soul, forcing her to confront the monster she had become. But she wouldn't break. She would

stand her ground. She would fight for her twisted sense of justice, even if it meant sacrificing her own freedom.

As the night deepened, the interrogators shifted tactics. They brought in a man with a calm demeanor, a soft voice, and a shrewd mind. He introduced himself as Dr. Bennett, a psychiatrist assigned to evaluate her mental state. His gaze was sharp, his smile unnerving. He spoke of her past, of her childhood trauma, of the darkness that simmered beneath her seemingly perfect exterior.

His words cut deep, peeling back
layers of carefully
constructed defense mechanisms. He
knew her, understood her, saw the
monster she had always been. He saw
the truth behind her manufactured
normalcy, the flicker of darkness in
her eyes that spoke of a primal need
for retribution.

The doctor's words were a siren call, a whisper of
possibility.
He offered a chilling ultimatum: join
the CIA, become a weapon against
other serial killers, or face a lifetime
behind bars. It was a choice between
two evils, a gamble with her own
soul.

Elsa stared at the man, her mind consumed by the weight of his offer. The prospect of freedom, of being a hunter, of wielding her dark impulses for a greater good, was intoxicating. Yet, the thought of becoming a tool, a weapon in someone else's twisted game, sent shivers down her spine.

She looked at the blood-soaked sheets, the grim reminder of her transgression. The fear was still there, the guilt gnawing at her edges. But a new feeling bubbled within her, a primal hunger, a thirst for power that seemed to drown out the fear.

She chose the darkness. She chose the hunt.

As the guards led her away, her mind was already spinning

with the possibilities. She was no longer just a monster. She was a weapon, a hunter, a force of darkness unleashed. And in that moment, she felt a strange sense of relief, a twisted sense of purpose. The world was a battlefield, and she was a soldier, a predator in a game of survival.

The Ultimatum

The sterile fluorescent lights of the interrogation room buzzed, casting a harsh glow on Elsa's face. It felt like a stage, the stark white walls amplifying the silence as she sat opposite the two men in suits. One, with a sharp jawline and a gaze that seemed to dissect her soul, was Agent Walker. The other, radiating an air of clinical detachment, was Dr. Maddox, the CIA's resident psychiatrist.

"We know what you did, Ms. Gardner," Agent Walker stated, his voice a measured baritone. He held a photograph, a blurred image of the bloodied man, his face twisted in agony. "We have the evidence, the witnesses. You'll be facing charges, a life behind bars."

Elsa's gaze remained steady. She had always been good at hiding her emotions, her face a mask of composure. The truth was, a part of her, a dark, twisting tendril, welcomed the prospect of prison. It was a cage, yes, but one that promised a twisted kind of security. But a flicker of something else, a spark of defiance, ignited within her.
"You're offering me a choice?"

Agent Walker leaned forward, his eyes cold and calculating. "We need people like you, Elsa. We need someone who can understand the twisted minds of the monsters out there, someone who can play the game, even if it means getting their hands dirty."

He paused, letting the weight of his words settle. "You have the skills, the instincts. You have a hunger for justice, albeit a twisted one. We can give you a purpose, a chance to use your darkness to fight the darkness."

Dr. Maddox, who had remained silent until then, spoke, his voice soft but firm. "We're offering you a chance to be a weapon, Elsa. But it comes with a price. We will monitor you, analyze your every thought, every impulse. You will be under constant scrutiny, your every move scrutinized. We will be watching you, Elsa, just as carefully as you watch your prey."

Elsa's gaze flickered between the two men, a silent battle playing out in her mind. The thought of a life behind bars, confined and controlled, was suffocating. But the promise of power, of becoming a predator hunting predators, was a seductive lure.

"I'll do it," Elsa finally spoke, her voice a low murmur, tinged with an unsettling calm. "But know this, I'm not playing by your rules. I'm taking what you offer, but I'm not sacrificing my own desires. I will hunt, I will kill, and I will do it my way."

A flicker of a smile crossed Agent Walker's face, a sharp, predatory grin. "That's the Elsa Gardner we know. Welcome to the fold, Ms. Gardner. Your training begins tomorrow."

The sterile room pulsed with the unspoken understanding of their pact. Elsa, a woman consumed by darkness, had traded her freedom for a taste of power. The CIA had gained a weapon, a hunter who understood the beast within. But in the heart of this exchange, in the chilling silence that followed, lurked a dangerous truth: Elsa had chosen the path of the predator, but she had also unleashed the very monster she was meant to hunt.

Her journey had begun, a descent into
the shadows of a world where
morality was a faded memory, and the
only rule was survival. And she, Elsa
Gardner, was ready to play.

The Training Ground

The air crackled with the scent of sweat and
anticipation.
Elsa stood before the imposing figure
of Agent Hayes, a veteran of the
CIA's most elite unit, his eyes like
cold steel beneath the brim of his
worn-out baseball cap. The training
grounds of Langley were a brutal,

unforgiving landscape, a testament to the Agency's dedication to forging its operatives into instruments of the shadows. This was where Elsa would learn to become a weapon against the darkness that she herself embodied.

The first weeks were a blur of grueling physical and mental trials, designed to push her to the very edge of her
endurance. Each day was a relentless cycle of combat
training, weapons handling, interrogation techniques, and psychological conditioning. Elsa embraced the challenge with an almost manic fervor, her past demons fueling her determination. She was a natural in the physical realm, her years of MMA training giving her a

brutal edge. But the mental tests were far more insidious, designed to probe the depths of her psyche, to see if the darkness she carried could be controlled, weaponized, or if it would ultimately consume her.

One day, Agent Hayes stood before her, a single, chilling line etched on his face. "We're going to test your capacity for empathy." He said it with a cold, detached tone, his voice a rasping whisper that seemed to seep into the very core of her being. She knew what that meant.

The next few days were a descent into a psychological labyrinth. Elsa was subjected to hours of interrogation

simulations, forced to confront
the horrors of real-life

crimes, their raw details projected
onto a screen, their
victims' faces etched with pain and
fear. The simulations were designed
to break her, to expose the cracks in
her
carefully constructed facade. To see if
the darkness within her would turn her
into one of the monsters she was
meant to hunt.

But Elsa was no ordinary recruit. The
trauma of her own past, the visceral
thrill of her own killings, had
hardened her, twisted her into a
weapon of her own making. She felt a

strange, perverse satisfaction in dissecting the psychology of each perpetrator, their motives, their methods, their twisted desires. The violence on screen, the raw pain and suffering, it was a morbid dance that resonated with something deep within her, a twisted symphony of chaos and control.

One night, after a particularly brutal simulation, Elsa found herself staring into the mirror of her tiny, spartan room, her reflection a stranger she barely recognized. The lines around her eyes were deeper, her gaze more intense, the corners of her lips twisted into a chillingly familiar smirk. She felt a strange sense of exhilaration, a fleeting thrill that came from knowing that she was on the verge of something dangerous, something exhilaratingly dark.

She could see the flicker of approval in Agent Hayes's eyes, the subtle acknowledgement of her potential, her willingness to embrace the darkness. The CIA was nurturing her, molding her into something formidable, a weapon against the very darkness that she held within.

Elsa knew that the life she had chosen was a path paved with blood and bone. She was walking a tightrope between redemption and self-destruction, and she was increasingly aware that the line between the two was becoming blurred with each passing day. But as she stood before Agent Hayes, the future stretching before her like a vast, uncharted ocean,

she couldn't help but feel a surge of adrenaline, a thrill that ran through her veins like a shot of pure, untainted power. The hunt was about to begin.

The Hunters Code

The air hung heavy with the scent of ozone and the stale tang of sweat, a grim reminder of Elsa's relentless training. Her muscles ached, her lungs burned, yet she pressed on, each repetition pushing her closer to the precipice of control. In this crucible of pain, she discovered a strange kind of peace. Here, in the unforgiving grip of physical exertion, her inner turmoil, the relentless echo of her past, seemed to fade into a distant hum.

"You're getting better, Gardner," a gruff voice broke the silence. It was Silas, her instructor, a former Special Forces operative with eyes that held the cold gleam of a predator. His gaze was sharp, piercing, dissecting her with every word. "But you're still too eager. Too impulsive. This isn't about blind vengeance, Elsa. It's about strategy, about reading the game before it even starts."

Elsa knew he was right. Her past had fueled her, but here, in the sterile confines of the CIA training facility, she was learning a new language, a language of control, a language of the hunter. Her instincts, the raw, primal hunger for retribution, were being refined, shaped into something more precise, more calculated.

Silas continued, his voice a low growl. "You have to understand the hunter's code. It's not just about catching the prey. It's about knowing its every move, anticipating its desires, its weaknesses. You have to become the darkness, Elsa, to understand the darkness."

This was the heart of the lesson, the chilling truth Silas was forcing upon her. To hunt the monsters, she had to become

one of them. She had to embrace the shadows, to delve into the murky depths of their twisted psyches, to understand the seductive allure of their monstrous desires.

Silas handed her a file. "Your first target. A man they call 'The Weaver.' He has a unique MO, meticulous, almost artistic in his execution. A serial killer who leaves his victims in

a state of ritualistic display, a
macabre tableau of death."

Elsa opened the file, her gaze
scanning the gruesome photos, the
detailed reports. The Weaver was a
master of deception, a puppeteer who
danced with death. His victims were
chosen meticulously, each one a piece
in his twisted game, a
testament to his warped sense of
control.

"He doesn't kill for pleasure, Elsa,"
Silas explained, his voice a chilling
whisper. "He kills for power. He
wants to control the narrative, to
manipulate the world around him. He
wants to be seen."

Elsa's fingers traced the photo of the Weaver's latest victim, a young woman left in a macabre pose, her body contorted into a chilling mockery of life. It was a horrifying spectacle, a testament to the killer's warped imagination.

"He needs to be stopped," Elsa murmured, a dark glint in her eyes. "But how?"

"You'll figure it out, Gardner," Silas said, his gaze unwavering. "You'll learn to think like him, to anticipate his moves, to become the predator."

The words hung in the air, heavy with unspoken promises, with the weight of a twisted destiny. Elsa's mind began to race, her analytical mind churning, dissecting the Weaver's past, his patterns, his methods. She felt a strange thrill

coursing through her, a dark satisfaction as she began to unravel his intricate web.

The Weaver was a puzzle, a twisted masterpiece of human depravity, and Elsa, the reluctant hunter, was determined to solve it. But as she delved deeper, she couldn't shake the unsettling feeling that the closer she got to understanding the Weaver, the more she felt the darkness within herself rise, a monstrous echo of the predator she sought.

The training was merely the first step, a gateway into a world of shadows and secrets, where the lines between hunter and hunted blurred, and the allure of the dark side whispered promises of power. Elsa knew that she was walking a razor's edge, a delicate balance between justice and her own twisted desires. But she was ready to dance with the devil, to play his game, and to win.

The first target had been chosen. The hunt had begun.

Elsa, the woman haunted by her own darkness, the woman who had embraced the hunter's code, was ready to face the monsters in the shadows, to confront the darkness within herself, and to walk the treacherous path of redemption.

The First Target

The air hung heavy in the sterile white room, a stark contrast to the vibrant hues of the city outside. Elsa, still adjusting to the unforgiving glare of the fluorescent lights, sat across from a man who exuded an aura of detached authority. His name was Dr. Alistair Blackwood, a psychiatrist assigned to monitor her every move, a silent observer of the darkness within her. His presence was a constant reminder of the deal she had made, a pact with the devil in exchange for freedom.

She glanced at the file in his hands, its cover emblazoned with the ominous seal of the CIA. It was a document that held the details of her first assignment, the first step on her path as a weapon against the very demons she embodied.
The words on the page blurred, her mind racing, caught between a chilling anticipation and a deep-seated fear. Her instincts, honed by years of suppressing her darkest urges, screamed at her to run, to disappear. But the promise of power, of controlling the darkness,

held her captive, a venomous lure she couldn't resist.

Blackwood cleared his throat, his voice a soothing yet unsettling baritone. "You've been chosen for a special program, Elsa. One that requires a unique set of skills –skills you possess in abundance." He paused, letting the implication hang in the air, a knowing smirk playing on his lips. "This program is designed to identify and neutralize individuals who exhibit a predilection for… unorthodox methods."

Elsa fought to maintain a stoic facade, her internal turmoil a storm raging beneath the surface. "And what kind of methods are we talking about, Doctor?" Her voice was a

whisper, laced with barely concealed menace.

Blackwood's eyes narrowed, his gaze piercing through her. "We're talking about serial killers, Elsa. Men and women who operate outside the confines of societal norms, driven by impulses most wouldn't dare comprehend."

Elsa felt a surge of adrenaline course through her veins. The thrill of the hunt, the intoxicating prospect of unleashing her own darkness on a worthy adversary, was a heady cocktail. She couldn't help but feel a flicker of perverse satisfaction. This was her domain, a realm of twisted desires and macabre games, a stage where she was not only the hunter but the hunted.

"Tell me about the target, Doctor," she demanded, her voice now a low growl, a primal instinct taking hold.

Blackwood smiled, a chillingly predatory expression. "He's a man named Gregory Hayes. His MO is… unique." He leaned forward, his voice dropping to a conspiratorial whisper. "He likes to create art with his victims, sculptures of flesh and bone, a macabre testament to his twisted vision.

He's a meticulous artist, a master craftsman of the human form."

Elsa's gaze sharpened, her senses tingling with a strange mixture of revulsion and excitement.
"What's his target profile?"

"He focuses on young, vulnerable women. He hunts them in the shadows, their screams silenced before they can even utter a cry for help."

"And where does he operate?"

"The city, Elsa. Our city. The same streets we walk, the same places we call home. He's a predator lurking among us, a ghost in the night."

Elsa felt a chill crawl down her spine. This was a game she knew, a dance she was all too familiar with. She could see his reflection in the darkness she carried within, a twisted mirror reflecting her own inner demons.

"Give me everything you have, Doctor," she commanded, her voice resonating with newfound purpose. "This is where my true work begins."

Blackwood nodded, his gaze never leaving hers, a silent agreement forged between two predators locked in a

macabre dance. He handed her a file
thick with details:
photographs, case reports, and a
chillingly detailed analysis of Hayes'
psychological profile. The pages were
a tapestry of macabre beauty, a
testament to the dark artistry of a man
consumed by his own twisted desires.

As Elsa delved into the file, she felt
the familiar thrill of the chase
awaken within her, a primal instinct
that had been dormant for too long.
The scent of blood, the promise of
vengeance, it was all coming back to
her, a seductive
symphony of darkness. This was
what she was born to do, what she
had always been destined to become:
a hunter, a predator, a weapon

against the very darkness that
consumed her.

The hunt had begun, a battle between two
predator minds.
And Elsa, the woman who had once
walked a tightrope between the law
and her own dark desires, was now on
the cusp of becoming something
more. She would hunt Gregory Hayes,
not just for justice, but for a twisted
sense of self-discovery, a quest to
unravel the complexities of her own
tortured soul.

The city streets stretched out
before her, a labyrinth of
shadows and secrets. She would

navigate this world, her heart pounding in sync with the dark rhythm of the hunt.

Elsa was no longer just a woman haunted by her past, she was a weapon, a tool of vengeance, a predator poised to claim her prey. And in the dark alleys, amidst the whispers of fear and the chilling echoes of violence, she would find her true purpose. The city, her playground, would become a canvas for a dance of death, a macabre performance starring her as the lead role.

The hunt for Gregory Hayes, the first target of her new life, had begun.

And Elsa, the woman who embraced her

darkness, was ready to play.

The Dance of Death

The air hung thick with the scent of decay and disinfectant, a potent cocktail that Elsa had come to recognize as the signature aroma of the CIA's training facility. She stood in the center of a mock crime scene, the sterile white walls echoing the emptiness in her soul. Across from her, a hulking figure with a shaved head and eyes that held the cold steel glint of a honed blade, played the role of a victim, his limbs contorted in a grotesque tableau of death.

This wasn't just another drill. It was an introduction to the world of serial killers, a twisted ballet where each move, each gesture, held a macabre significance. Elsa had spent the past weeks immersed in a world of twisted minds, their pathologies mapped out in detail, their desires laid bare like anatomical specimens. She had studied their MO's, the meticulous choreography of their killings, the rituals they enacted, the dark fantasies that fueled their actions.

But this wasn't about understanding them. It was about becoming them.

"Focus on the details," the instructor's voice rasped,
breaking the silence. "The blood spatter, the way the body is positioned, the angle of the blade. Each detail is a story, a window into

the killer's mind. You must learn to see it, to feel it."

Elsa, her eyes narrowed, took a step closer to the staged body. Her gaze, sharp and calculating, lingered on the crimson stains that painted the walls, the way the victim's fingers, frozen in a desperate attempt to fight back, still clutched at the fabric of his shirt. The instructor's words

echoed in her mind, a chilling mantra.

"The killer leaves a signature. Not just in the way they kill, but in the way they orchestrate the scene, the messages they leave behind."

Elsa felt a familiar surge of anticipation, the thrill of the hunt weaving through her veins. This was the language she understood, the language of violence, the language of the predator and the prey.

The training facility was a macabre labyrinth, a twisted mirror that reflected the darkness within her. The walls were lined with displays of disturbing artifacts – photographs of crime scenes, meticulously preserved evidence, instruments of torture. Each object whispered its own story, a chilling testament to the depravity of human nature.

Elsa felt a strange sense of kinship with these horrors. They were a language she understood, a language she had begun to speak long before she was forced to embrace her fate.

The instructors, hardened veterans of the CIA's shadowy world, pushed her relentlessly, driving her to the limits of her physical and mental endurance. They honed her skills, refining her already formidable arsenal. She learned to wield weapons with deadly precision, her movements honed by years of MMA training, her mind a battlefield where strategy and instinct waged a constant war. She learned to read body language, to detect subtle shifts in behavior, to sense the dark impulses that lurked beneath the surface.

Elsa embraced the role of the hunter, embracing the darkness that had always been a part of her. She reveled in the power she wielded, the control she exerted over her own destructive impulses, the knowledge that she held the power to inflict pain and death, to deliver a twisted form of justice.

But as the weeks turned into months, the shadows that clung to her began to shift, to take on a more sinister hue. The thrill of the hunt, once a potent intoxicant, began to lose its allure. She started to see the stark reality of her actions, the faces of her victims, the despair that mirrored the emptiness in her own heart.

One afternoon, during a particularly grueling session, the instructor, a man with piercing blue eyes and a haunted gaze, stopped her in the middle of a simulated fight. His voice, devoid of emotion, shattered the silence.

"You're losing control," he said, his words like ice shards piercing the air. "The darkness is consuming you. You need to find a way to manage it, to control it, or it will consume you."

Elsa's heart hammered against her ribs, the chilling truth of his words echoing through her.

"I'm in control," she spat back,
her voice laced with defiance.
"This is who I am. I'm a
weapon. A tool."

The instructor shook his head, his expression
unreadable.

"You may be a weapon," he said,
his voice soft but firm. "But you
are also a human being. And
human beings are capable of
great evil."

His words lingered in the air, a silent
accusation that echoed in the
chambers of her soul. The emptiness
she had been so determined to fill

with violence, with the power of her own darkness, had only grown more vast, more profound.

Elsa's world had become a twisted game, a macabre dance with death, where every move, every decision, carried a

dangerous weight. The line between hunter and hunted blurred, and the darkness that she had embraced threatened to consume her entirely. The dance of death had begun, and Elsa was both the choreographer and the dancer, caught in a deadly waltz with her own inner demons.

The Confrontation

The air hung heavy with the scent of stale coffee and fear. It was a peculiar mix, one that Elsa had grown accustomed to in the sterile, dimly lit room where the CIA had deemed it necessary to house her. Her hands, calloused and scarred from years of martial arts training, tightened around the ceramic mug, the heat a fleeting comfort in the cold, clinical environment.

This was her first assignment, the culmination of months of rigorous training and a twisted bargain struck with the agency. A serial killer, they called him, a predator stalking the city's darkest corners, leaving a trail of victims in his wake. They had chosen her, Elsa Gardner, the woman who knew darkness intimately, to hunt him.

His MO, they explained, was intricate, almost poetic. He collected victims, meticulously chosen, and staged their corpses in elaborate tableaux, each scene a macabre work of art, a haunting testament to his warped mind.

"He's a puzzle," the handler, a man named Agent Reed, had said, his eyes reflecting a chilling understanding of the darkness that lurked beneath the surface. "And you, Elsa, are the key to solving it."

He had called her the "Hunter," a title she felt ill-equipped to wear. The word felt like a mask, a flimsy veil concealing the monstrous truth she carried within. But there was a thrill in the hunt, a dangerous energy that coursed through her veins. It was a thrill that echoed the intoxicating rush she had felt after her first kill, a dark symphony that played on repeat within her soul.

Elsa studied the dossier on her target, a man named Thomas Blackwood, a name that resonated with a chilling familiarity.

His face, a pale mask of normalcy, was the only clue she had, a face that could easily blend into the throngs of ordinary people. He was a chameleon, a predator who moved unseen, unheard, leaving only a trail of terror in his wake.

Days blurred into weeks, a relentless pursuit that consumed her every thought. The city felt different, the air thick with a palpable tension that she could sense in the shadowed corners of alleyways and the vacant stares of strangers. The city was a canvas, Blackwood's work of art, each victim a brushstroke, a chilling testament to his twisted genius.

Her pursuit took her through the underbelly of society, a world of smoke-filled dives and back alleys, where whispers carried secrets and fear was the currency of the streets. She spoke to informants, listened to their tales of the "Blackwood" terror, piecing together the fragments of a horrifying puzzle. Each piece she uncovered revealed another layer of darkness, a deeper understanding of the predator she hunted.

Then came the lead, a tip from a drug-addled informant who claimed to have seen Blackwood. He had been seen frequenting a dilapidated warehouse on the city's fringes, a place where the city's forgotten ghosts wandered in the shadows.

Elsa felt a flicker of anticipation, a primal instinct awakening within her. This was it, the moment she had been waiting for, the culmination of her relentless pursuit. The warehouse loomed before her, a concrete behemoth shrouded in darkness. The air hung heavy with the scent of decay, a testament to the neglect and secrets it held.

She moved through the shadows, her senses on high alert, her mind racing. The warehouse was silent, a tomb of concrete and steel, the echoes of her footsteps the only sound breaking the oppressive stillness. She found herself in a vast, cavernous space, filled with an unnerving emptiness that seemed to amplify the silence.

And then, she saw him.

Thomas Blackwood stood in the center of the space, his back turned, his silhouette illuminated by a single flickering bulb overhead. He was a study in contradiction, his ordinary clothes a stark contrast to the morbid art that surrounded him.

"Blackwood," Elsa spoke, her voice a low growl. The name felt foreign on her tongue, a word imbued with the weight of death and darkness.

He turned, his face a mask of calm as he met her gaze. "Elsa Gardner," he said, his voice a low rumble. "The CIA's newest weapon."

He seemed to know her, not just by name, but by the darkness that resided within.

"You're not the first hunter I've encountered," he said, his voice a mocking whisper. "You're not the first to think you could understand the shadows."

He took a step towards her, his eyes boring into her soul. "But you are the most intriguing."

There was a spark of recognition in his gaze, a chilling echo of the darkness she had buried deep within. He knew her, understood her, in a way no one else ever had.

"It's not about understanding," Elsa said, her voice a chilling monotone. "It's about stopping you."

The warehouse pulsed with tension, the air thick with unspoken threats. The silence hung heavy, a palpable anticipation of violence. Elsa knew that what she was about to do was wrong, morally reprehensible. Yet, she felt a strange sense of liberation, a release of the darkness she had suppressed for so long.

She took a step forward, her hands moving with the practiced grace of a predator.

The confrontation was inevitable,
a dance of death
choreographed by two predator
minds. It was a clash of darkness,
a battle between two souls
intertwined by their shared hunger
for a world shrouded in shadows.

And in that moment, as the hunter
and the hunted locked eyes, Elsa
realized that the lines she had so
carefully drawn were blurring, the
darkness she had sought to conquer
was becoming a part of her, a twisted
symphony echoing in her soul.

The Psychiatrists Gaze

The sterile, white walls of the psychiatrist's office felt like a tomb. Elsa perched on the edge of the plush leather chair, her gaze fixed on the man across from her, a man who held a chilling power over her. Dr. Silas Thorne was a beacon of calm amidst the storm raging within her. His gentle eyes seemed to pierce through her meticulously crafted facade, analyzing every twitch of her muscles, every subtle shift in her expression.

"Elsa, how are you feeling today?" Thorne's voice was a soothing balm, but it did little to ease the turmoil churning in her gut. The weight of her recent actions, the brutal acts of revenge that had become a twisted dance, pressed heavily on her. The guilt, she'd convinced herself, was a necessary price for the satisfaction of ridding the world of its rot. Yet, under Thorne's watchful gaze, her convictions faltered.

Elsa's voice was a low rasp, barely audible above the hum of the air conditioner. "I... I'm fine." Her words were a lie, a carefully woven fabrication to mask the darkness that threatened to consume her. Each breath felt like a struggle against the suffocating shadows that clung to her.

Thorne leaned forward, his keen eyes never leaving hers. "You've been having nightmares again, haven't you?" He spoke with a quiet certainty that left no room for denial.

Elsa flinched. Thorne had a way of peeling back her layers, exposing the raw, vulnerable core she desperately tried to protect. Her dreams, a chaotic tapestry of blood and screams, were a constant reminder of the horrors she'd inflicted. She'd chosen to be a hunter, a weapon against the darkness, but the

line between predator and prey had become dangerously blurred.

"It's just... stress," she mumbled, trying to force a semblance of composure.

Thorne's lips curved into a knowing smile, a subtle flicker of amusement in his eyes. "Stress? Elsa, you're the one hunting the monsters, the one wielding the blade. You're the one who should be beyond stress."

She bit her lip, the sting of his words a sharp reminder of her carefully crafted façade. She'd embraced the darkness, allowed it to consume her, but the darkness wasn't simply a tool. It was a serpent, twisting and coiling around her,
whispering promises of power and retribution.

"I... I'm just trying to do what's right," she said, the words sounding hollow, even to her own ears.

Thorne's eyes softened, a flicker of sympathy in their depths.

He understood her, not in a way that sought to judge or condemn, but in a way that acknowledged the darkness that resided within her, a darkness he recognized in himself. He had been chosen for this role, the one who delved into the minds of the most dangerous individuals, the one who walked the tightrope between sanity and madness.

"What is right, Elsa?" Thorne asked, his voice a quiet whisper. "Is it the satisfaction of vengeance, the thrill of the hunt, or something deeper, something you haven't yet fully acknowledged?"

Elsa's heart hammered in her chest, the force of his question sending tremors through her. She couldn't answer him. She didn't know the answer. She'd been so consumed by the darkness, by the need for retribution, that she'd lost sight of

the true motives behind her actions.

"What drives you, Elsa?" Thorne persisted, his voice steady, unwavering. "What makes you chase these monsters, these echoes of your own darkness?"

The question hung heavy in the air, a challenge to her carefully

constructed justifications. She couldn't escape the truth anymore. She had been chosen for this role, just as Thorne had been, but there was a chilling, almost seductive truth hidden within her. She craved the violence, the power that came with it, the raw thrill of hunting, the primal
satisfaction of taking a life.

Elsa's gaze dropped to her hands, the knot of tension tightening in her stomach. She knew Thorne saw through her, saw the monster she'd embraced, the one who had always lurked beneath the surface.

"It's not about justice," she whispered, the admission a breath of cold air.

"It's... it's about something else."

Thorne's eyes held a mixture of understanding and sadness. He had seen this darkness too often, in himself and in others.
It was a dangerous path, a slippery slope, and the descent was often inevitable.

"What is it, Elsa?" Thorne's voice was a gentle nudge, a coaxing whisper. He was leading her closer to the truth, to the core of her being.

"It's… I need to feel alive," Elsa admitted, her voice cracking under the weight of the truth. "I need to feel like I have some control, some power. It's a hunger, a need that never goes away."

Thorne nodded slowly, a flicker of understanding in his eyes.

He knew the feeling. It was the same darkness that had fueled his own descent into the depths of the human psyche. But he had chosen to become a shepherd, a guide, a beacon of hope amidst the shadows.

"And you think taking lives, hunting these monsters, is the only way to satisfy that need?" Thorne asked, his voice tinged with a sense of both sympathy and warning.

Elsa's gaze fell to the floor, the
weight of her actions
crushing down on her. She couldn't
deny it. The killings, the hunt, they
filled a void, a primal need she didn't
understand.

"I don't know," she whispered, her
voice barely audible. "I just… I just
need to stop it, stop the violence."

"But you don't," Thorne said, his
voice a gentle, but
unwavering, counterpoint. "You keep
going back to the shadows, to the
hunt. You crave the violence, Elsa.
You can't deny it."

Elsa looked at him, the weight of his
words pressing down on her. She

knew he was right. She couldn't escape the truth.
She was a predator, a creature of darkness, and she had embraced the darkness, had let it consume her.

The session ended with a heavy silence. Elsa walked out of the office, the weight of Thorne's words a heavy burden on her shoulders. She was a hunter, a weapon against the darkness, but the darkness had become a part of her, a dangerous, seductive force that threatened to consume her.

Elsa knew she had to change, to find a way to control the darkness within her, but the path to redemption was unclear. The shadows were tempting,

the violence alluring, but she had to find a way to break free, to find a way to be
something more than a predator. The journey was long, the

path fraught with danger, but she had to try. She had to find a way to reclaim her humanity, to escape the darkness that threatened to devour her.

The Shadow of Doubt

The sterile white walls of the CIA psychiatrist's office felt like a tomb, a stark contrast to the chaotic symphony of emotions raging within her. Elsa, a woman sculpted from darkness, had been molded into a weapon, a hunter of killers, but the line between predator and prey was becoming increasingly blurred. Her hands, once instruments of precision and violence, trembled slightly as she stared at her reflection in the polished surface of the coffee table. The once-familiar face, now etched with the scars of her deeds, seemed alien to her.

She had tasted the blood of her victims, the intoxicating power of taking a life, and it had left an indelible mark on her soul. The psychiatrist, a man who peered into the abyss of her psyche, had become a constant presence, a reminder of the facade she had built. He saw through her carefully crafted mask, recognizing the monster lurking beneath the surface. His questions were like daggers, piercing her defenses, forcing her to confront the chilling truth she had buried deep within.

The weight of her past deeds was a crushing burden. The memory of her first kill, the cold-blooded execution of a college classmate, haunted her dreams, a constant reminder of her descent into darkness. She had convinced herself that it was justice, a righteous act against a perceived injustice, but now, as she stood on

the precipice of her twisted reality,
the justifications began to crumble.

The CIA had embraced her darkness,
harnessing her
monstrous instincts to hunt down
other predators. She was a weapon, a
tool for good in their eyes, but in her
heart, she

felt the insidious whispers of her
own demons. They whispered of
power, of the thrill of the chase,
and the seductive allure of her
own darkness. They were a siren's
call, beckoning her towards the
abyss.

She had become a master of disguise, a chameleon blending seamlessly into the shadows of the city, but it was a lonely existence. The trust she had once cherished had become a fragile illusion, a fragile bridge over the abyss that

threatened to swallow her whole. The world she knew, the world she had fought so hard to maintain, was slipping away, replaced by a chilling reality where lines blurred and morality was a distant memory.

The psychiatrist's questions echoed in her mind, relentless and probing, forcing her to confront the unsettling truth of her existence. His gaze was unsettling, a constant reminder of the power he wielded, the ability to dissect her very soul. He asked her

about her motives, her justifications, but the answers eluded her. The truth was a tangled web of twisted desires, buried under layers of self-deception and the
intoxicating lure of her own darkness.

As she sat in his office, trapped in a silent battle with her own demons, a wave of nausea washed over her. The cold, clinical setting of the psychiatrist's office felt suffocating, a stark contrast to the brutal world she had become
accustomed to. The scent of antiseptic and the quiet hum of the air conditioner seemed to amplify the disquiet within her.

The memories of her victims, their faces etched in her mind, were a constant reminder of the horrors she had inflicted.

She could feel their presence, their pain, their anger, a chilling echo of the darkness that had consumed her. They were a heavy weight on her soul, a constant reminder of the price of her choices.

Elsa, the woman who had become a weapon against evil, was now wrestling with the very evil that resided within her. She was a hunter, but she was also the hunted, trapped in a cage of her own making. The line between justice and vengeance had become a blurry abyss, and the consequences of her choices were becoming increasingly apparent.

She had been a predator, a force of destruction, but now, a glimmer of doubt had taken root in her mind. The validity of her twisted sense of justice was being questioned, the foundation of her self-justification crumbling beneath her.
She was a woman on the precipice of a descent into
darkness, the shadows of her past threatening to engulf her whole.

Elsa's eyes, once bright and unwavering, now held a flicker of fear, a desperate hope for redemption. She had tasted the blood of her victims, the intoxicating power of taking a life, but the thrill was fading, replaced by a gnawing sense of guilt and the chilling realization that she had become a monster. She was a woman caught in a cruel game, forced to confront the darkness that resided within her, the monster she had become.

The Weight of Guilt

The weight of guilt pressed down on Elsa like a physical entity, a constant companion that never left her side. It was a heavy cloak woven from the chilling memories of her victims, their faces etched into the fabric of her mind, their screams echoing in the caverns of her soul. She couldn't escape them, not even in her dreams. They were always there, their presence a tangible reminder of the horrors she had inflicted.

The goose, its lifeless body a testament to her youthful darkness, was a recurring nightmare. The image of the bird's terrified eyes, wide with fear as she tightened her grip on its neck, was forever burned into her memory. The goose had been her first kill, a reckless, impulsive act fueled by a childish fascination with death, a morbid curiosity that had spiraled into something far more sinister. It had been a taste of power, a glimpse into the intoxicating abyss of her own nature, and it had left her craving more.

Then there was the college classmate, a perceived injustice fueling her rage. She had plotted and planned, meticulously constructing a facade of normalcy while her inner demons whispered promises of retribution. The act itself, the execution of a carefully laid plan, had been exhilarating, a twisted validation of her self-proclaimed sense of justice.

The aftermath, however, had been far less satisfying. The guilt had crept in, a venomous serpent coiling around her heart, slowly poisoning her soul. She had tried to ignore it, to bury it beneath layers of rationalization and justification, but the truth remained a

festering wound, a constant reminder
of the monstrous darkness that lurked
within.

Now, with the CIA looming over her,
the weight of her past deeds
threatened to crush her. The
psychiatrist, Dr. Alistair Thorne,
watched her with an unsettling
intensity, his keen eyes probing the
depths of her psyche, seeking to
understand the monstrous desires that
fueled her. He was a constant
reminder of the scrutiny she was
under, the fragile facade she had built
to mask her true nature. He knew the
truth, or at least a part of it, and the
unsettling knowledge of his

awareness added another layer to the burden of her guilt.

Each time she slipped on a fresh mask, a new persona to fit the demands of her new mission, the echoes of her past echoed back to her. The victims, their faces forever etched in her memory, whispered accusations of her deeds. Their pain, their fear, their screams, were a constant chorus that haunted her every waking moment. She had embraced the darkness, chosen the path of the hunter, but the darkness had embraced her back, leaving its indelible mark on her soul.

She was trapped in a perpetual cycle of self-destruction, a puppet master dancing on the razor's edge of redemption and self-annihilation. With each kill, she sought to exorcise her own demons, to find a twisted form of solace in the destruction she inflicted upon others. But the more she killed, the more the weight of her guilt pressed down on her, the more the whispers of her past haunted her, reminding her of the chilling truth - she was not a hero, she was a predator.

The darkness that resided within her was not a monster to be hunted, it was a part of her, a twisted reflection of her own being. She had become a weapon against the very darkness that consumed her, and the more she wielded that weapon, the more the darkness bled into her, threatening to drown her in the abyss of her own guilt.

The psychiatrist, with his penetrating gaze and endless questions, served as a mirror to her own soul. He forced her

to confront the reality of her actions, to acknowledge the monstrous truth of her own nature. He saw through the layers of her carefully constructed façade, the carefully crafted justifications she used to mask her true motivations. He saw her not as a weapon, but as a victim, a prisoner of the darkness that consumed her.

The struggle for control was a constant battle, an internal war that raged within her every waking moment. The darkness within her whispered promises of power, of satisfaction, urging her to embrace the monster she had become. But the weight of her guilt, the haunting echoes of her past, pulled her back from the precipice, reminding her of the human cost of her choices.

She was a monster, a predator, a hunter of darkness, but she was also a woman, a flawed creature struggling to find her place in a world that had long since rejected her. The more she hunted, the more she realized the truth - she was not saving the world, she was merely a reflection of the darkness she sought to destroy. And as the weight of her guilt pressed down on her, she wondered if there was any way to escape the darkness she had embraced, any way to find redemption for the sins she had committed. The answer remained elusive, a flickering beacon of hope in the endless sea of her own despair.

The Struggle for Control

The antiseptic smell of the CIA's psychological evaluation room clung to Elsa's skin like a second layer, a constant reminder of the cage she was trapped within. She sat across from Dr. Alistair Thorne, his gaze piercing, searching for the monsters lurking beneath the surface of her carefully constructed facade. She had been assigned to him, a psychiatrist tasked with monitoring her every move, a silent guardian against the darkness she embraced.

Elsa's eyes, a storm of jade and midnight, held a flicker of defiance. She knew Thorne saw right through her, his keen intellect a threat to the delicate balance she had maintained for so long. He delved into her past, a relentless explorer charting the map of her twisted psyche. Each session was a confrontation, a game of chess where her secrets were the pawns and Thorne the ruthless strategist.

He pressed, a tireless interrogator seeking to unravel the threads of her justifications, the twisted logic she used to rationalize her actions. He knew the truth – the thrill of the hunt, the intoxicating power of extinguishing life, the darkness that resided within her soul. It wasn't just the killings; it was the control, the artistry, the cold calculation that fueled her hunger.

The memories clawed at her, the faces of her victims a haunting chorus in her mind. The goose, its lifeless eyes a chilling reminder of her childhood fascination with death.

The college classmate, a pawn in
her twisted game of revenge. The
man who had assaulted her
roommate, a predator brought to
justice by her own hand. Each
kill, a brushstroke on the canvas
of her darkest desires.

Elsa fought back, her mind a fortress
of razor-sharp
defenses. She deflected his questions,
weaving narratives that showcased her
as a savior, a righteous predator
cleansing the world of evil. She
painted herself as a soldier, a warrior
battling the monsters that lurked in the
shadows, a hero in a world devoid of

heroes.

But Thorne wasn't fooled. He saw
the subtle tremors in her hands, the
fleeting flicker of guilt in her eyes.
He knew the guilt wasn't for her
victims; it was for the woman she
was losing, the fragments of
humanity she was leaving behind.

"Elsa, you are a contradiction," he
spoke, his voice a gentle caress that
carried the weight of steel. "A brilliant
mind, a skilled predator, a woman
who walks a tightrope between
darkness and light. You convince
yourself that you are doing good,
ridding the world of monsters. But are
you not, in your own way, the monster
you hunt?"

Elsa flinched, the question a poisoned arrow striking a vulnerable nerve. She had built her entire world on this delicate balance, the illusion of justice a shield against the monster she carried within. Now, Thorne, with his unyielding gaze and his unnerving understanding of her soul, threatened to shatter that illusion.

She tried to answer, to spin a narrative that would deflect his piercing observation. But the words caught in her throat, choked by the truth that he so effortlessly unearthed. She knew the truth, the ugly, unfiltered truth of her own nature. The monster she hunted was a reflection, a twisted mirror image of the darkness that resided within her.

The battle raged within her, a war
between the predator she had
become and the remnants of
humanity she desperately clung to.
The darkness, a seductive whisper,
promised

power, control, and a perverse sense
of justice. But the faint flicker of
light, a beacon in the vast ocean of
her darkness, reminded her of the
woman she had once been, the
woman she was slowly losing.

She couldn't fight it, not anymore. The
line between hunter and hunted had

blurred, the predator she sought to destroy mirrored in the depths of her own soul. She was a monster, a creature of darkness with the power to destroy, but also a woman capable of love, compassion, and a desperate yearning for redemption.

Elsa's eyes met Thorne's, a silent exchange of understanding. He saw her struggle, the war raging within her, the fragile balance that threatened to shatter. He knew, as she did, that the monster she hunted was a part of her, a constant companion in the labyrinth of her twisted soul.

"I am not the monster, doctor," she said, her voice a strained whisper. "I am the one who hunts them."

But even as she spoke, a flicker of doubt danced in her eyes, a silent acknowledgment of the truth she couldn't deny. She was both hunter and hunted, a creature of darkness caught in the eternal cycle of predation, a twisted testament to the human capacity for both monstrous cruelty and desperate redemption.

The Price of Power

The steel of the interrogation room felt cold against Elsa's back, even through the layers of her CIA-issued jacket. Dr. Harris, her ever-present psychiatrist, sat across from her, his gaze a piercing probe into her soul. He wasn't a man who flinched from the darkness, but a man who sought to understand it, to dissect it, to tame it. He wasn't the first to try, and likely wouldn't be the last.

"Elsa," his voice was calm, measured, a soothing balm on the storm that raged within her, "how do you feel about your recent assignment?"

The memories flickered before her eyes, vivid and brutal, a kaleidoscope of blood and terror. She'd caught the killer, a man who orchestrated elaborate, twisted games with his victims, a predator who reveled in the fear he instilled. The hunt had been exhilarating, a dance on the edge of the abyss.

"I... I did what I had to do," she said, her voice barely a whisper. It felt hollow, echoing the hollowness within her.

Harris leaned back, his eyes narrowed in observation. "And what do you have to do, Elsa? You're a skilled hunter, an assassin, a weapon. But what's the price of that power?"

He was right. The price was steep, a constant gnawing ache in the pit of her stomach, a weight that pressed down on her soul. The isolation, the constant scrutiny, the knowledge that she walked a razor-thin line between justice and oblivion – it was a burden she carried with each kill.

The guilt wasn't a constant, oppressive force. It came in

waves, crashing over her in the quiet moments, when the adrenaline faded and the echoes of screams lingered in the darkness. It was in the glimpses of her reflection, the cold, detached gaze that stared back at her, a stranger she barely recognized anymore. It was in the dreams, where the faces of her victims swirled around her, their accusing eyes burning into her soul.

"The price?" she repeated, her voice trembling slightly. "The price is a part of me I can't get back, a part of me I'm not sure I want back."

Harris didn't press, his silence a heavy blanket suffocating the room. He understood. He was the one who saw the fissures in her facade, the cracks in her carefully constructed reality. He knew the darkness she sought to control, the darkness that gnawed at her from within.

"It's a lonely path, Elsa," he finally said, his voice laced with a hint of pity. "The line between justice and vengeance is a thin one. How much longer can you walk it?"

Elsa looked away, unable to meet his gaze. She couldn't answer him. She didn't know how much longer she could walk this path. With each kill, the darkness within her grew, its tendrils creeping further, threatening to consume her whole.

The world outside was a blurry canvas, a chaotic symphony of noise and motion. But within her, the storm raged, fueled by the memories of her victims, the chilling whispers of their despair. She was a weapon, a hunter, a creature of the night, and the price of her power was a soul she was slowly losing.

"There are other ways," Harris said softly, his voice a gentle breeze against the raging storm within her.

"Ways to find peace, to find redemption."

His words were like a lifeline, a glimmer of hope in the suffocating darkness. But she knew it wasn't that simple. She had embraced the darkness, and it had embraced her back. Could she ever truly escape its grasp?

The interrogation room felt smaller, suffocating. The steel felt cold against her skin, a constant reminder of the prison she had built for herself. The price of power, she realized, was more than just the loss of innocence, it was the loss of herself.

She looked at Harris, his eyes filled with concern and a flicker of something else, something akin to sorrow. She saw a reflection of herself in his gaze, a woman who had become a stranger to herself.

"Perhaps you're right," she said, her voice strained, a whisper lost in the echoing silence. "Perhaps there are other ways."

But even as the words left her lips, she knew she was lying. The darkness had seeped too deep, its tendrils entwined with her very being. She was a hunter, and her prey was the darkness within her own soul.

She might seek redemption, but
the price she had paid for power
was one she would have to carry
forever.

The Return to Innocence

The air hung thick with the scent of
damp earth and decaying leaves, a
pungent aroma that clung to the air
like a shroud. Elsa stood at the edge of
the clearing, her gaze fixed on the
spot where her first kill had taken
place. It was a place she had vowed

never to return to, a painful reminder of the abyss that yawned within her soul. Yet, here she stood, the past pulling her back into its icy grip.

A shiver ran down her spine, not from the cold but from the visceral memory of that night. She could almost see him again, the young man, his face contorted in terror as he begged for his life. The memory was so vivid it felt like a nightmare replaying in her mind, the cold glint of the knife, the sickening thud of his body hitting the ground, the surge of adrenaline that had coursed through her veins.

It had been a long time since she had thought about that night, since she had allowed herself to dwell on the raw, primal thrill of taking a life. She had buried that part of herself, shoved it deep down into the recesses of her mind, where it lay dormant, like a venomous serpent coiled in the darkness. Now, the memory had resurfaced, unbidden, a phantom limb reminding her of the darkness she carried within.

She took a step forward, the crisp autumn leaves crunching under her boots, a jarring sound that shattered the silence of the clearing. The air seemed to hold its breath, as if sensing the weight of the past that hung heavy over this place. She closed her eyes, trying to shut out the images that flooded her mind, the fear, the guilt, the exhilarating sense of power that had enveloped her that night.

As she stood there, a wave of nausea washed over her, a physical manifestation of the emotional turmoil that raged within. It was a feeling she hadn't experienced in years, a stark reminder of the monster she had become. She had learned to suppress her emotions, to compartmentalize the darkness she carried within. But here, in this place, the walls she had so carefully constructed crumbled, revealing the raw, unfiltered truth of who she was.

A single tear rolled down her cheek, tracing a path through the dust and grime that had collected on her face. It was a tear of remorse, of regret, of the deep-seated guilt that gnawed at her soul. She had never been one for sentimentality, for allowing emotions to cloud her judgment. But in this moment, the weight of her actions bore down on her, crushing her with a force that threatened to break her in two.

She felt a strange sense of longing, a yearning for the innocence she had once possessed, the innocence that had been so brutally ripped away from her. She remembered the warmth of her grandmother's embrace, the comfort of her childhood home, the simple joys that had once filled her life. It was a world that felt impossibly distant now, a world that she had traded for a life steeped in darkness.

The world had been so black and white back then, she had thought, the lines between right and wrong clearly defined. But life had a way of turning those lines into blurry shades of gray, a cruel lesson she had learned the hard way. She had crossed that line, stepped into the darkness, and now she couldn't find her way back.

Her gaze fell upon the small, weathered tombstone that stood at the edge of the clearing, a testament to the life that had been taken here. The name carved on the stone, a simple inscription, brought back a flood of memories, a wave of remorse that threatened to drown her.

She reached out, her fingers tracing the cold, smooth surface of the stone, feeling the chill seep through her gloves. It was a connection to a past she could no longer escape, a tangible reminder of the path she had chosen and the life she had taken.

As she stood there, lost in the depths of her memories, a voice echoed through the silence. A voice that sounded eerily familiar, whispering words that pierced through the fog of her thoughts.

"You can't run from your past, Elsa," the voice hissed. "It's a part of you, woven into the fabric of your being."

Elsa turned slowly, her gaze searching the clearing, but she saw no one. The voice seemed to emanate from the very trees, from the air itself, a ghostly presence that had come to haunt her. It was a voice that sounded strangely like her own, a voice that spoke of the dark secrets she kept buried deep within.

She took a deep breath, trying to steady her nerves, to banish the chilling whisper that had pierced through her composure. She told herself it was her imagination, a product of the dark memories that tormented her. But deep down, she knew the voice was real, a reflection of the monster she had become.

The voice continued, its words slithering through the silence, a serpent's hiss that sent shivers down her spine. "You can't hide from who you are, Elsa. You are a hunter, a predator, a monster. Embrace your true nature."

The words were a stark indictment, a cruel echo of the truth she had been trying to deny. She had tried to justify her actions, to convince herself that she was doing good, that she was a force for justice. But the voice, the voice that echoed from within her own soul, told a different story. It spoke of the darkness that resided within her, the insatiable hunger for violence that fueled her every move.

Elsa closed her eyes, trying to shut out the voice, to silence the whispers that threatened to consume her. But they were too powerful, too persistent, too real. The voice, a reflection of her own inner darkness, had become a tangible entity, a force that she could no longer deny.

She opened her eyes, her gaze fixed on the tombstone, the inscription a stark reminder of the consequences of her actions. She knew, with a chilling certainty, that she could never escape the darkness that clung to her. It was a part of her, woven into the very fabric of her existence, a truth she could no longer ignore.

She took a step back, turning away from the tombstone, from the past that haunted her. She couldn't escape the darkness, but she could choose how to live with it. She had chosen a path, a twisted path that had led her to this point, a path that would forever shape her destiny.

With a heavy sigh, she turned and walked away, leaving the clearing behind, the chilling whispers of the past fading into the distance. The air was cold, the wind biting, a harsh reminder of the darkness that had consumed her. But within that darkness, she could feel a flicker of hope, a spark of something that refused to be extinguished.

She was a monster, yes, but even monsters can find redemption. And she, Elsa Gardner, the hunter, the predator, the woman who had embraced the darkness, was not done fighting yet. She had a long way to go, a long road to walk before she could even begin to understand the monster she

had become. But she would keep fighting, she would keep searching, she would keep hoping, for a chance to find a glimmer of light in the abyss that had become her world.

The Scars of Memory

The air hung heavy with the stench of mildew and the
metallic tang of old blood. It was a scent that clung to Elsa's memories, a ghostly echo of her past. She stood before the dilapidated barn, the scene of her first kill, a place she had sworn never to return to. The rusty hinges of the barn door creaked like a dying

animal, a sound that sent shivers down her spine, a shiver that wasn't just from the cold but from a deeper, more unsettling source.

The years had stripped the barn of its vibrant red paint, leaving behind a skeletal facade, a symbol of decay mirroring the decay of her soul. Inside, the floor was littered with hay, now matted and damp, a silent testament to the horrors it had witnessed. The air was thick with the phantom smell of fear and the metallic tang of blood. It was a sensory assault, a symphony of darkness playing on her nerves.

As Elsa stepped inside, memories flooded her mind. She saw herself, a younger, more innocent Elsa, standing before her victim. She saw the panic in the boy's eyes, the desperate plea for mercy that had only fueled her resolve. She saw the glint of the knife in the flickering light, the way it danced in her trembling hand, a dance of death that she could never escape.

And then, the rush. The primal surge of adrenaline, the intoxicating thrill of power, and the chilling sense of control. The boy's blood splattered on the barn floor, a crimson stain that seemed to burn itself into her consciousness. But the thrill soon faded, replaced by a creeping dread, a chilling realization of the irreversible act she had committed. The echoes of the boy's screams, the haunting image of his lifeless eyes, they were all locked in her memory, a constant reminder of the monster she had become.

As she walked through the barn, a cold wind swept through the cracks in the wooden walls, a ghostly whisper that sent a wave of nausea through her. Each creak of the floorboards, each rustle of the hay, seemed to echo with the memory of her first kill, the brutal act that had irrevocably shattered her innocence.

She moved towards the hayloft, the place where she had dragged the boy's body, a final act of cruelty that only intensified her horror. As she climbed the rickety ladder, her hands trembled, the cold wood sending shivers through her fingers. The loft, once a place of hay and dreams, was now a chilling reminder of her descent into darkness.

Standing in the center of the loft, she closed her eyes, forcing herself to confront the memory. The stench of blood, the cold, the crushing weight of guilt. It all rushed back, overwhelming her senses, threatening to drown her in the abyss of her own darkness.

A deep, guttural growl escaped her lips, a sound that tore from her throat, a raw expression of the anguish she had been trying to suppress for years. It was a sound that resonated through the barn, a primal scream of pain and rage. She was a wolf trapped in a cage, consumed by the darkness within, unable to escape the echoes of her past.

This was not the first time she had revisited this place, this dark, cursed barn. She had returned countless times, seeking answers, seeking a way to understand the monstrous desires that consumed her. But each visit only deepened the darkness within, solidifying the chilling truth that her actions were not born from justice, but from a twisted sense of power, a primal urge to inflict pain.

Her memories weren't just confined to the barn. They were scattered across the city, each place etched with the memory of her victims, each street a haunted corridor leading back to the dark abyss of her soul. Every alleyway whispered
secrets, every shadow concealed a chilling truth. And in the silence of the night, the city echoed with the ghostly
whispers of her victims, their voices a constant reminder of the darkness she carried within.

The city was a reflection of her own twisted mind, a
labyrinth of darkness and deceit where morality was a fading memory and the boundaries of sanity were constantly blurred. She was a predator, a hunter,

a monster who stalked the streets, a reflection of the shadows she carried within.

The weight of her past, the burden of her sins, it pressed down on her like a leaden weight, a constant reminder of the choices she had made, the darkness she had embraced. It was a darkness that threatened to consume her, to shatter her sanity and drag her into the abyss of her own making. She had walked a tightrope between justice and vengeance, balancing on the razor-thin edge of redemption and self-destruction. And the weight of her choices, the consequences of her actions, they threatened to pull her down into the abyss.

The city of angels, as it was so proudly called, was a facade, a mask that hid the darkness that festered beneath the
surface. And Elsa was the embodiment of that darkness, a woman haunted by her own twisted desires, a woman who had embraced the monster within, and in doing so, had become a chilling testament to the darkness that lay hidden in the hearts of all men.

The Burden of Truth

The scent of pine needles and damp earth filled Elsa's lungs as she stood on the edge of the clearing. The air was thick with the memory of a crisp autumn day, the same day she had taken the life of her first victim. It was an act of

vengeance, she told herself back then, a way to right a wrong that had left her feeling violated and powerless. But now, standing amidst the fallen leaves, a chilling realization pierced through her carefully constructed facade.

The truth, cold and stark, settled into her gut like a lead weight. Her desire for justice, the righteous anger that had driven her to murder, it was all a mask. A shield she had used to deflect the true nature of her desires, the darkness that pulsed within her like a second heartbeat. The thrill of the hunt, the intoxicating power of taking a life, it was these that had driven her, not some lofty sense of morality. She was a predator, a monster masquerading as an angel of justice.

It was in the aftermath of that first kill that she felt a fleeting sense of exhilaration, a twisted satisfaction that left her both disgusted and strangely exhilarated. The guilt, the horrifying realization of what she had done, it was a fleeting emotion, overshadowed by the intoxicating rush of power. She had tasted blood, and the taste, the sensation, it had left her craving more.

This craving, this insatiable hunger for violence, had been with her since she was a child. The memory of a young Elsa, standing over the lifeless body of a goose, her face stained with blood and a sense of detached awe in her eyes, this memory was a stark reminder of her inherent darkness. She

had always had a morbid fascination with death, a morbid fascination that had blossomed into something more sinister, a twisted sense of pleasure in the act of taking a life.

The years that followed, her seemingly normal college life, the carefully cultivated image of a studious, responsible young woman, it was all a facade. A carefully crafted mask to hide the monster lurking beneath the surface, the monster that craved to be unleashed. It was a world of shadows and secrets, a world where she could indulge in her darkest desires, where she could be the hunter, the executioner.

Now, standing in the clearing, surrounded by the echoes of her past, she realized that she had been playing a dangerous game. A game where the lines between justice and vengeance blurred, a game where she had become the very evil she sought to destroy.

She was a monster, no doubt about it. She was a predator, driven by a darkness that pulsed within her, a darkness that had always been a part of her. But could she escape this darkness, could she find a way to atone for her sins? Or would she forever be trapped in a cycle of violence, a creature of the night, forever haunted by the echoes of her past?

The questions gnawed at her, the weight of her actions bearing down on her like an unbearable burden. She wasn't sure if she could bear the weight of it all, not anymore. The truth had a way of breaking you, of stripping you bare, leaving you exposed and vulnerable. She was broken, a shattered mirror reflecting the monster she had become.

But even in the face of this daunting truth, a spark of hope flickered within her. A sliver of light in the darkness, a whisper of redemption. Perhaps, there was a way, a way to atone, a way to break free from the cycle of violence that had

defined her. Perhaps, she could find a way to be more than the monster she had become.

She looked up at the sky, a vast expanse of bruised purple, a reflection of the turmoil within her. The first stars had begun to appear, twinkling like distant promises. There was still time, she thought, still time to find a way to escape her darkness.

And so, she took a step back, a slow, deliberate step away from the clearing, away from the ghost of her past. The scent of pine needles and damp earth lingered in her nostrils, a reminder of the darkness she carried within. But there was a new scent now, too, a faint whisper of hope, a promise of a different path.

Elsa walked away, a predator with a flickering spark of redemption in her eyes, a woman haunted by the echoes of her past, yet determined to find a way to escape its grip. Her journey had just begun, a journey through the labyrinth of her own soul, a journey towards the uncertain, yet hopeful, light of redemption.

The Search for Redemption

The fluorescent lights of the abandoned warehouse pulsed like a sickly heartbeat, casting harsh shadows that danced across the concrete floor. Elsa stood in the center of the cavernous space, the echo of her own footsteps amplifying the oppressive silence. This was the place, the scene of her first kill, the place where the innocence of her youth bled out into the cold, calculating darkness she had embraced. It was a place of raw, primal memories, a haunting reminder of the path she had chosen.

The air was thick with the scent of dust and decay, a tangible manifestation of the forgotten horrors that clung to this space. Elsa closed her eyes, the scene flashing before her inner vision – the fear in her victim's eyes, the metallic tang of blood, the chilling thrill that had coursed through her veins. She remembered the exhilaration, the sense of power that had taken root in her soul. She had been a predator, a hunter in a game of her own making. But somewhere between the thrill of the kill and the cold reality of her actions, a sliver of doubt had taken root. It had grown, a persistent whisper in the back of her mind, questioning the validity of her choices, the justification for her descent into darkness.

She had chosen the path of the hunter, a weapon against the darkness that plagued society. She had embraced the role, honing her skills with a ruthless efficiency, driven by a twisted sense of justice. Yet, as she stalked the shadows, her own darkness began to consume her, its tendrils reaching into the deepest recesses of her psyche. Her victims became more than just targets, they became reflections of her own inner turmoil, echoes of the violence that resided within her.

The facade she had so carefully crafted began to crack, revealing the monster she had become.

Elsa opened her eyes, the harsh glare of the fluorescent lights momentarily blinding her. The image of the psychiatrist's watchful gaze flickered in her mind, his questions probing the depths of her soul, his skepticism a constant reminder of her fractured reality. He was a man who saw through her carefully constructed facade, a man who understood the monstrous desires that fueled her actions. He was a mirror, reflecting the darkness she desperately tried to hide.

She ran a hand through her hair, the gesture a nervous tic, a testament to the turmoil raging within her. She had become a hunter, a predator, but the line between her and the monsters she hunted had blurred. She was no longer a woman who walked the razor's edge of morality, she had fallen into the abyss, consumed by the darkness she sought to destroy.

The echoes of her past reverberated through the warehouse, each sound a reminder of her descent. The memories, once buried deep within her psyche, now clawed their way to the surface, a relentless torrent of guilt and shame. Her first kill, the one that had opened the floodgates to her darkness, haunted her with a terrifying clarity.

Elsa felt a cold dread grip her heart as she relived the scene, the image of her victim's lifeless eyes a stark reminder of the horrors she had inflicted. She had justified her actions, told herself she was bringing justice to a world consumed by evil.

But in the cold light of day, the truth was inescapable. She was a murderer, a monster who reveled in the thrill of violence.

The path she had chosen was leading her deeper into the abyss, a downward spiral fueled by her insatiable desire for retribution. The monsters she hunted reflected her own inner

demons, her every act a validation of the darkness that
consumed her. She was a prisoner of her own making,
trapped in a cycle of violence that threatened to consume her entirely.

Elsa knew she had to find a way to escape the darkness, a way to atone for the sins she had committed. The path she had chosen was leading her to destruction, but there was a flicker of hope, a faint glimmer of redemption in the distance.

The memories of her childhood, the traumatic events that had ignited her primal instincts, surged to the forefront of her mind. They were the seeds of violence, the foundation upon which her darkness had grown. She

remembered the
betrayal, the injustice, the searing pain
that had ignited a fire within her, a fire
that had consumed her entire being.

Elsa's childhood had been a crucible,
forging her into a weapon, a force of
retribution. She had learned to
suppress her emotions, to embrace her
rage, to channel her pain into a
destructive force. She had believed
she was seeking justice, that she was
making the world a better place by
ridding it of evil. But the truth was far
more complex.

Her actions were driven by a deep-
seated need for control, a need to
right the wrongs that had been
inflicted upon her. But in her quest
for vengeance, she had become the

very thing she sought to destroy. She had crossed the line,
blurring the boundaries between justice and retribution.

Elsa closed her eyes, the weight of her past pressing down on her with a crushing force. She was a monster, a creature of darkness, a woman consumed by her own demons. But within the abyss of her soul, there was a sliver of hope, a whisper of redemption.

She knew she couldn't continue down the path she had chosen. The darkness was consuming her, her actions becoming increasingly erratic, her morality eroding with each passing day. She had to find a way to escape the cycle of violence, a way to find peace and atonement.

The warehouse stood as a stark reminder of her descent, a monument to the horrors she had inflicted. But it was also a place of reflection, a place where she could confront the demons that haunted her, the monsters she had become. She had to find a way to face the truth, to confront the reality of her actions, and to seek a path toward redemption.

The air in the warehouse was heavy with the weight of her past, but Elsa could feel a shift within her. A spark of hope, a glimmer of light, was beginning to emerge from the darkness. It was a small flame, but it was a start, a sign that she was not entirely lost.

Elsa knew she had a long and difficult journey ahead of her, but she was finally ready to face it. She had to confront the horrors she had inflicted, to atone for her past, and to find a way to redeem herself. It wouldn't be easy, but she had to try.

The future was uncertain, but she was determined to find a path out of the darkness, a way to escape the monster she had become.

As she turned to leave the abandoned warehouse, the echo of her footsteps reverberated through the cavernous space, a testament to the weight of her past. But there was something different now, a subtle shift in the air, a whisper of hope in the darkness.

Elsa knew she still had a long way to go, but she was no longer alone in her struggle. She had found a glimmer of light, a beacon guiding her towards redemption.

The path ahead was uncertain, but she was determined to find her way back from the abyss, to find a semblance of peace in the wreckage of her past.

The Choice

The air hung heavy with the scent of damp earth and decay, a sickly sweet perfume that clung to the back of Elsa's throat.

She stood at the edge of the overgrown lot, the skeletal remains of the old factory looming behind her like a rusted monument to her past. The memory of that night, crisp and vivid, played out in her mind like a macabre film.

The adrenaline, the thrill of the kill, the intoxicating sense of power that had coursed through her veins. It had been her first, the moment she truly embraced the darkness within. Now, as she stood before the scene of her crime, she felt a strange mix of regret and morbid fascination.

It wasn't the guilt that gnawed at her, not really. It was the realization that the violence, the bloodlust, was woven into her very fabric. It wasn't a choice she made, but a part of who she was, an echo of her past that reverberated through her every waking moment.

A harsh laugh escaped her, dry and hollow. It had been a simple case, a routine act of revenge against a man who had wronged her. But it had been the turning point, the catalyst that sent her down this twisted path.

She had been a bright, ambitious student, destined for a career in criminal justice. But the darkness had always simmered beneath the surface, a primal instinct that gnawed

at the edges of her consciousness.
The encounter with that man, the
betrayal, the sense of powerlessness,
had ignited the flame.

She'd chosen to silence him, to take his life, to
right the

wrong in her own twisted way. And
the thrill of it, the
intoxicating sense of control, had left
her both exhilarated and terrified. It
was a taste of power she craved, a
hunger she couldn't ignore.

Her reflection in the grimy window
of an abandoned
storefront stared back at her. The

shadows played tricks on her face, twisting her features into something sinister. Her eyes, once vibrant with youthful hope, now held a cold, calculating gleam.

She could see the darkness swirling within, a vortex of violence and desperation. It was a part of her she could no longer deny, no longer hide. But the question lingered, heavy and suffocating: was this all she was? Was she merely a monster, a predator driven by primal urges?

The echo of Dr. Vance's voice rang in her ears, his calm, measured tone cutting through the chaos in her mind. He'd warned her of the darkness, the insidious nature of the violence. "It's a slippery slope," he'd said, his eyes filled with a mixture of concern and a chilling understanding. "Once you embrace it, it consumes you."

Elsa had dismissed his warnings, brushing them aside with a haughty air. She was in control, she thought. She was a weapon, a tool of justice, ridding the world of its most dangerous predators. But the truth was, she was no different from the killers she hunted.

She felt a shiver run down her spine, a chilling sensation that made her blood run cold. She wasn't a hunter; she was a predator, a creature of the night, fueled by a thirst she couldn't quench.

The memory of her first kill, the sickening reality of the aftermath, the lingering stench of blood and fear, it all came

flooding back. The guilt, the shame, the horrifying realization that she had embraced the very darkness she sought to eradicate.

She could feel the echoes of the past resonating within her, a constant reminder of the path she'd chosen. It was a path that led to a chilling crossroads: embrace the darkness fully, become the monster she hunted, or find a way to break free from its seductive allure.

It was a choice that haunted her dreams, a battle she fought within the confines of her own mind. And as she stood there, the shadows of the abandoned factory closing in around her, she knew she could no longer ignore the choice that lay before her.

Elsa took a deep breath, trying to find some semblance of calm amidst the whirlwind of emotions that raged within. Her heart beat a frantic rhythm, a drum solo in the silence of the night. She had to choose, a choice that would determine her fate, a choice that would define her very essence.

But the question remained, a chilling echo in the back of her mind: was there any turning back? Was there any hope for redemption, or was she forever bound to the darkness that consumed her?

With a shuddering breath, she turned away from the scene of her first kill, her gaze fixed on the horizon, a faint glimmer of hope in the distance. The choice was hers to make, and the weight of it pressed down on her like a physical burden. And as she walked away, she couldn't help but feel a sense of foreboding, an unspoken fear that she might be lost to the darkness forever.

The New Hunt

The sterile white walls of the CIA headquarters felt more like a prison than a sanctuary. Elsa sat at her desk, her fingers drumming a restless rhythm against the polished surface. The scent of coffee lingered in the air, a weak attempt to mask the metallic tang of fear that permeated the atmosphere. Her eyes, dark and bottomless, were fixed on the file in front of her. It contained the details of her latest case, a serial killer with a particularly disturbing MO, a killer whose methods reflected a darkness that resonated with the shadows within her own soul.

The victim, a young woman named Emily, had been found in a secluded park, her body carefully posed, a

macabre display of artistry. Each
fingernail painted a different shade of
red, a twisted reflection of the crimson
that stained her skin. The killer had
left a calling card, a single crimson
rose placed between Emily's lifeless
fingers, a chilling signature that sent a
shiver down Elsa's spine.

A wave of nausea washed over her,
the familiar pang of both revulsion
and fascination. The killer's
meticulous attention to detail, the
calculated nature of his crimes, it was
all too familiar. It mirrored her own
twisted impulses, the dark desires that
had haunted her since childhood.

Elsa felt a tremor of unease, a
prickling sensation that
warned of a dangerous connection, a

reflection of her own darkness staring back at her from the pages of the file. The line between hunter and hunted had blurred, and Elsa found herself captivated by the killer's mind, drawn to the echo of her own twisted desires in his actions.

She studied the photographs, each gruesome detail a puzzle piece in the twisted game of their minds. The way the victim's eyes stared blankly, the unnatural stillness of her limbs, it was all too familiar, a disturbing echo of her own past deeds.

The psychiatrist, Dr. Harding, had warned her about this.

He'd cautioned her about the dangers of becoming too

invested in the cases, of allowing the darkness to consume her. But Elsa, fueled by her hunger for power and a twisted sense of justice, had dismissed his concerns. Now, she found herself grappling with the chilling reality of her actions, questioning the blurred lines between justice and vengeance.

Elsa knew that her own dark impulses were always lurking beneath the surface, a predator caged by the facade of

normalcy she had meticulously crafted. But now, with this new case, she felt a crack in the wall of her carefully

constructed self, a sense of unease that

gnawed at her sanity.

The killer's MO had a chilling familiarity to it, a macabre artistry that resonated with the dark impulses she had always kept at bay. The way the victims were posed, the symbols left behind, it all whispered of a twisted mind, a mind that mirrored her own in its fascination with death.

The hunt had begun, and Elsa, caught in a psychological battle with a reflection of herself, felt the weight of her own darkness pressing down on her. The fear that had always shadowed her, the chilling realization that she was not so different from the monsters she hunted, it all swirled around her, threatening to consume her entirely.

She knew she had to maintain her
control, to stay focused on the task at
hand. But the lure of the darkness was
strong, its seductive whispers
tempting her to embrace the predator
within. The line between hunter and
hunted was becoming

increasingly blurred, and Elsa, caught
in a dangerous game with her own
reflection, was losing sight of the path
she was meant to walk.

The Blurred Lines

The air in the sterile, white room crackled with tension, thick enough to choke. Elsa sat across from Dr. Silas, his kind eyes holding a disconcerting depth. He'd been a constant in her life since the CIA had plucked her from the brink of a life sentence, his probing questions and clinical observations a constant reminder of her fractured psyche. His gaze was a searchlight, illuminating the darkest corners of her soul, exposing the monstrous desires that lurked beneath the
surface of her carefully cultivated persona.

The case they were discussing now was particularly unsettling. The killer, known only as "The Architect," had a meticulous MO. He carefully staged his victims, constructing macabre scenes that were both artistically brutal and deeply disturbing. The police were baffled, the press frenzied. But for Elsa, the case had a chilling familiarity. There was a disturbing resonance, a twisted echo of her own past, of the meticulously planned, self-righteous acts of vengeance that had become her personal brand of justice.

"You see a reflection of yourself in this killer, don't you, Elsa?" Dr. Silas' voice was quiet, the words carefully chosen. His gaze never faltered, his keen intellect dissecting her every reaction. Elsa's gut clenched. She hated the way he saw through her facade, the way he could so effortlessly dissect her carefully crafted lies.

She met his gaze, a flicker of defiance in her eyes. "I'm a hunter, Dr. Silas. I'm not a monster like him." But the words felt hollow, even to her own ears. The line between hunter and hunted had always been blurred, a fragile membrane that threatened to disintegrate with each kill. It was becoming

increasingly difficult to distinguish between the righteous fury that fueled her and the cold, calculating pleasure she felt in the act itself. Was she a predator seeking to cleanse the world of evil, or was she simply a monster wearing the mask of justice?

"You may think you're different, Elsa, but your methods are becoming... disturbingly similar. The way you orchestrate these kills, the meticulous planning, the... satisfaction you derive from them. It's all mirroring The Architect's pattern, and I fear it's only a matter of time before you become indistinguishable from the monsters you hunt." His words were a cold shower, forcing her to confront the truth she'd been desperately trying to ignore.

"You're wrong," she spat, her voice tight with barely suppressed anger. "I don't enjoy the killing. It's a necessary evil, a means to an end. I'm doing what needs to be done."But as the words tumbled from her lips, they sounded like a desperate plea, an attempt to convince herself as much as him. Doubt, like a creeping vine, was beginning to strangle the foundation of her justifications.

The hunt for The Architect was proving to be far more challenging than Elsa had anticipated. He was a master of disguise, a chameleon who blended seamlessly into the mundane, leaving no trace of his presence except for the gruesome spectacle of his victims. Elsa found herself becoming increasingly obsessed with catching him, her pursuit fueled by a dark desire to understand the twisted mind that mirrored her own.

She spent countless hours poring over the crime scenes, analyzing the carefully constructed tableaux, the macabre theater of death he had orchestrated. The more she delved into his work, the more she felt a chilling sense of recognition, a disturbing echo of the darkness that had

always resided within her. The line between fascination and morbid identification became dangerously thin, a fragile barrier that threatened to shatter with each passing day.

One afternoon, in the secluded depths of her apartment, Elsa stared into a shattered mirror, the fragments reflecting a distorted image of her own face. Her reflection was a mask of contradictions, a mixture of beauty and ferocity, a delicate fragility juxtaposed against a chillingly calculated gaze. Was this the monster she hunted, the predator she so readily condemned? Or was she merely a reflection of the darkness she sought to eradicate?

As the days bled into weeks, the hunt consumed her. Her obsession with the Architect grew into a consuming fire, a relentless need to uncover the mystery that lurked within his twisted mind. The lines between her own psyche and his became hopelessly blurred, the boundaries of her own reality crumbling under the weight of her fascination.

She felt a strange kinship with the killer, a twisted sense of understanding that sent a shiver of dread down her spine. She had always believed that she was different, that her dark impulses were born out of a need for justice, a desperate attempt to make sense of the cruelty she had witnessed. But now, staring into the shattered fragments of her own reflection, she couldn't shake the feeling that she was staring at a monster.

And the monster, for the first
time, seemed to be staring back.

The Moral Compass

The city was a tapestry of neon and
shadows, a labyrinth of human
desires where darkness thrived. Elsa,
a predator cloaked in the anonymity
of the night, navigated the
treacherous terrain, her senses
heightened, her mind a
whirlwind of conflicting emotions.
She was a weapon, a hunter, a

woman trained to dismantle the twisted machinery of serial killers, but the very nature of the beast she hunted haunted her, mirroring the monstrous impulses that simmered within her own soul.

Her latest target, a man named Silas, was a reflection of her own darkness, a twisted mirror that distorted her perception of morality. He was a meticulous sadist, a puppeteer who reveled in the pain and humiliation of his victims, his crimes a calculated symphony of violence and control. With each detail of his crimes that unfolded, Elsa felt a creeping sense of familiarity, a recognition of her own twisted desires. It was as if Silas was a projection of her inner demons, a manifestation of the darkness she had so carefully hidden beneath a mask of normalcy.

She traced his movements, his every step a tantalizing clue, leading her deeper into the heart of the city's underbelly. The thrill of the chase was a drug, a heady concoction of adrenaline and morbid fascination. She reveled in the
adrenaline rush, in the power she wielded as she stalked her prey. But beneath the surface of this intoxicating rush lurked a gnawing fear, a creeping doubt that chipped away at her carefully crafted facade.

Each time she closed in on Silas, a familiar question echoed in the back of her mind: was she truly hunting a monster, or was she chasing a reflection of her own monstrous impulses? The lines between justice and vengeance blurred, and the boundaries of her own moral compass crumbled with each step she took. The world outside was a reflection of the chaos that raged within her, and the pursuit of Silas was becoming a dangerous descent into the abyss of her own psyche.

The psychiatrist, Dr. Elias, her appointed guardian, a man who sought to understand the darkness that drove her,
became a source of both comfort and conflict. He watched her, analyzed

her, piecing together the fragmented pieces of her past. But his attempts to penetrate her carefully constructed walls only served to amplify the internal battle raging within her. Elsa, skilled at deception, felt a twisted sense of triumph as she outwitted him, playing a dangerous game of manipulation, blurring the lines between reality and delusion.

The city pulsed with a dark energy, a palpable tension that mirrored Elsa's own internal turmoil. The neon lights, the ceaseless traffic, the throngs of people - it was all a facade, a mask concealing a raw, primal world of violence and despair.
And Elsa, a predator disguised as a hunter, was at the heart of this urban jungle, a woman poised

between redemption and self-destruction.

The weight of her past, the chilling memory of her victims, haunted her with a constant reminder of the horrors she had inflicted. Her first kill, the calculated execution of a college classmate, was a scar etched onto her soul, a constant
reminder of the path she had chosen. With each kill, with each life she took, the line between hunter and hunted blurred, leaving her in a state of perpetual unease, a prisoner of her own darkness.

She yearned for redemption, for a way to atone for the sins

she had committed. But the path she had chosen, the path of the hunter, was a one-way street, a descent into a world where the line between right and wrong had become hopelessly obscured. As she delved deeper into Silas's twisted world, she saw fragments of her own reflection, the darkest corners of her soul staring back at her with a chilling familiarity.

One night, as she tracked Silas through a labyrinth of back alleys and abandoned buildings, the city seemed to hold its breath. The air was thick with anticipation, the silence broken only by the echo of her own racing pulse. She knew she was closing in on her prey, but as she drew closer, a chilling realization dawned upon her - she was not just hunting a monster, but staring into a reflection of her own twisted self.

Elsa, the hunter, was losing her grip on the fragile line that separated her from the darkness. The world outside was a reflection of the chaos within her, and the lines between right and wrong had become hopelessly blurred. In the twisted reflection of Silas's crimes, she saw a reflection of her own descent, a haunting reminder of the monstrous impulses that lurked beneath the surface.

The hunt was becoming a journey of self-discovery, a dangerous descent into the abyss of her own psyche. The city, once a neutral ground, was now a battlefield, a reflection of the internal war raging within her. She was losing herself in the chase, becoming the very monster she was trying to destroy. And the question that haunted her, that gnawed at the core of her existence, was no longer: was she hunting a monster? It was: was she the monster?

The Doubting Mind

The fluorescent lights hummed, casting a sterile glow on the stark white walls of Dr. Miller's office. It felt like a prison cell, only instead of bars, the confines were invisible, woven from the threads of psychological scrutiny. Elsa, perched on the edge of the leather couch, felt like a specimen under a microscope, her every twitch, every flicker of emotion dissected, analyzed, and dissected again.

"You're making progress, Elsa," Dr. Miller said, his voice a soothing balm in the stark white world. "You're starting to connect the dots, to see the pattern in your choices."

Elsa felt a prickle of unease at his words. Progress? What kind of progress was he talking about? Did he not see the twisted logic that fueled her actions? The calculated dance of retribution, the twisted sense of justice

that had become her guiding
principle?

"I don't see it as a pattern, Dr.
Miller," Elsa countered, her voice
laced with a quiet defiance. "I see it
as a necessary evil, a way to right
the wrongs that plague this world."

He leaned forward, his gaze
unwavering. "And what about the
wrongs you've committed, Elsa? The
lives you've taken in the name of
justice? Are they not wrongs as
well?"

The words cut through her like a
scalpel. She had become so immersed
in the world of darkness, in the
righteous anger that propelled her

actions, that she had almost forgotten the collateral damage. The echoes of her victims, their fear and pain, their lives snuffed out in the name of her twisted sense of justice.

"They were monsters, Dr. Miller," Elsa said, her voice dropping to a whisper. "They deserved what they got."

"And who decides who deserves what, Elsa?" Dr. Miller asked, his voice a gentle, yet insistent, probe into her psyche.

"Do you truly believe you have the right to judge life and death?"

She looked away, her eyes tracing the intricate pattern of the carpet, a reflection of the tangled web of her own mind. The question echoed in the silence, reverberating against the walls of her carefully constructed facade. It was a question she had been grappling with for years, a question that
gnawed at her conscience, a question that threatened to unravel the very foundation of her reality.

"What if it's not real, Dr. Miller?" she whispered, the words barely audible. "What if this whole thing, this world, this…this game we're playing…what if it's all a twisted illusion?"

Dr. Miller didn't flinch, his gaze steady and unwavering. He simply waited, letting her words hang in the air, letting the weight of her doubt settle in the silence.

"There are times," Elsa continued, her voice gaining a tremor of urgency, "when I feel…like I'm slipping. Like the world around me is shifting, morphing into something…something unreal. Like I'm trapped in a nightmare, unable to wake up, unable to escape."

The words tumbled out, each one revealing a crack in the armor she had built, a crack that threatened to widen into an abyss. She was losing her grip, the boundaries between her reality and the dark recesses of her mind blurring with each passing moment.

"What makes you feel that way, Elsa?" Dr. Miller asked, his voice laced with concern. "What triggers these…these feelings of unreality?"

Elsa struggled to articulate the chaos that swirled within her, the inexplicable sense of disorientation that had begun to permeate her existence. The shadows that danced in the corner of her vision, the whispering voices that seemed to emanate from nowhere, the unsettling feeling that she was somehow observing her own life from a distance, detached from the very fabric of reality.

"It's like…like I'm watching myself," Elsa said, her voice trembling. "I'm here, in this room, talking to you, yet I feel…separated from it all. Like I'm observing it from a distance, like a detached observer, watching a scene unfold without any real connection to it."

Dr. Miller leaned back in his chair, his eyes fixed on her with a mixture of concern and intrigue. "And what do you see when you observe yourself, Elsa? What do you see in this detached observer?"

She closed her eyes, the image of herself, a distant, cold, almost inhuman figure, flickering in her mind. She saw the hunger in her eyes, the unwavering resolve, the chilling efficiency with which she executed her targets. She saw the darkness that had become an inextricable part of her being, the darkness that she had embraced, the darkness that had ultimately consumed her.

"I see a monster," she whispered, the truth finally breaking through the layers of denial, the fear and shame twisting in her gut. "I see someone who's lost all sense of reality, someone who's lost themselves in a world of shadows and violence."

The words hung heavy in the air, a confession of her deepest fears, a testament to the chasm that had opened within her.
She had become the very thing she hunted, a predator, a monster, consumed by a twisted sense of justice, and now, the very foundation of her reality was crumbling, leaving her adrift in a sea of doubt and uncertainty.

"Is that what you see, Dr. Miller?" Elsa asked, her voice barely a tremor. "Is that what you truly believe I am?"

Dr. Miller did not answer immediately, his expression unreadable. He simply sat there, observing her, studying the raw vulnerability that had finally breached her carefully constructed defenses. He saw the fear, the confusion, the desperation in her eyes, a reflection of the internal battle she was waging against the darkness that threatened to consume her.

"I don't know what you are, Elsa," he finally said, his voice calm and steady. "But I do know that you're in a great deal of pain, and that you need help."

Elsa's eyes met his, a flicker of hope igniting within her. In the darkness of her own mind, in the relentless spiral of doubt and self-loathing, she had almost forgotten that there was someone who could see her pain, someone who might offer her a glimmer of hope in the face of the abyss.

The battle had just begun, and the war within her was far from over. But for the first time, she felt a flicker of hope, a faint glimmer of light piercing the darkness that threatened to engulf her.

The Descent

The rain hammered against the grimy window of the CIA safe house, mirroring the storm brewing within Elsa. She hadn't slept in two nights, the phantom echoes of the last case clinging to her like a shroud. It had been a symphony of madness, a gruesome ballet of pain and despair orchestrated by a man who called himself "The Weaver." His victims, all young women, were found arranged in macabre tableaux, their bodies intertwined like threads in a morbid tapestry.

Elsa had traced his movements, his twisted logic, felt a chilling kinship in the cold, calculated precision of his crimes.

But there was a darkness within The Weaver that resonated with a primal fear in Elsa, a dark reflection of her own hidden abyss. She couldn't shake the feeling that she was staring into a warped mirror, one that showed her own potential for utter depravity. Every kill, every gruesome scene she'd witnessed, every whisper of her own monstrous desires, had chipped away at the fragile facade she'd built, leaving her clinging to the precipice of self-destruction.

Dr. Vance, her psychiatrist and self-proclaimed guardian of her sanity, had noticed the shift. His eyes, usually placid and observing, had begun to hold a flicker of concern, almost fear. She could see it in the way he held her gaze a beat too long, the way his fingers tapped nervously against the table during their sessions. He knew, she was certain, that the hunter was starting to become the hunted. He was witnessing her slow, insidious descent into the very darkness she was tasked with conquering.

Tonight, the storm within her was reaching a crescendo. She

couldn't escape the whispers in her mind, the primal urges clawing at the edges of her sanity. They had become a constant companion, a chorus of whispers that urged her to embrace the chaos, to indulge in the raw power of

destruction. She knew she was

walking a razor-thin line, the line

that separated control from complete

and utter ruin.

The phone rang, a shrill, insistent

interruption to her internal turmoil. It

was a call from her handler, a voice

devoid of emotion, informing her of a

new case. A single, chilling sentence:

"The Butcher of Beacon Hill is on the

move

again."

Elsa's grip tightened on the phone.

The Butcher of Beacon Hill. A

notorious serial killer who targeted

young men, his signature being

meticulously clean, surgical-like

dismemberment. He was a ghost in

the city, a phantom of terror that had haunted the streets for years, leaving behind a trail of fragmented bodies and shattered lives.

She had always felt a certain detached fascination with The Butcher. His calculated brutality, his surgical precision, it was a perverse form of artistry that both repulsed and
intrigued her. She knew he was a monster, a predator who reveled in the terror he instilled. But there was something within him, a spark of darkness that resonated with the shadows within her own soul.

"Elsa," the voice on the phone said, its tone laced with an undercurrent of caution, "We need you on this. The

Butcher's MO is escalating, and the city is on edge."

"The Butcher," she whispered, the name a mantra, a whisper of a siren song. "He's a masterpiece, isn't he?"

The handler's voice remained emotionless. "Elsa, focus. You're needed."

She closed her eyes, the rain drumming on the window a relentless rhythm of her inner chaos. "I'm coming," she whispered, her voice a hollow echo of the storm raging within her. "I'm coming to play."

The hunt was on. The game had begun. And Elsa, the predator within, was ready to unleash her own brand of twisted justice.

The city lights, a glittering tapestry of neon and darkness, reflected in the rain-slicked streets, mirroring the distorted reflection within Elsa's own soul. The line between hunter and hunted blurred, the world around her morphing into a twisted maze of shadows and whispers. Each step she took drew her deeper into the abyss, and she was no longer certain whether she was pursuing the monster, or if the monster was already consuming her from within.

The next few days were a blur of adrenaline, obsession, and the intoxicating allure of the chase. She poured over case files, meticulously piecing together the Butcher's history, his habits, his perverse patterns. Each detail she uncovered, each fragmented clue, fueled her obsession, pulling her further into the vortex of her dark obsession.

The Butcher had left his calling card - a single, crimson rose left at the foot of each victim, a macabre symbol of his
twisted artistry. Elsa kept one of these roses on her desk, a memento of her prey, a tangible link to the world of macabre she had become intimately

familiar with. The petals, once a vibrant crimson, were now stained with the residue of her own twisted desires.

She knew she was losing herself, the line between good and evil, between justice and retribution blurring beyond
recognition. The constant pursuit of monsters had begun to

twist her own perception of reality, warping her sense of self and morality. Her psychiatrist's warnings echoed in her mind, a faint whisper of reason amidst the cacophony of chaos. But the allure of the hunt was too strong, the intoxicating power of the chase too potent.

One evening, late into the night, Elsa was poring over a case file, her eyes scanning the grim details of The Butcher's latest victim. The victim's name, James Carter, barely registered in her mind. All she saw were the gruesome details of his death, the intricate patterns of the dismemberment, the chilling artistic precision.

She looked down at the crimson rose on her desk, its thorns a reminder of the razor-thin line she walked. The room seemed to close in on her, the walls pressing against her, suffocating her with the weight of her own darkness.

"Elsa," a voice broke the silence, a gentle, almost hesitant voice. Dr. Vance stood in the doorway, his face etched with concern. He hadn't been to the safe house in days, but something in his eyes told Elsa that he knew she was in trouble.

"What are you doing here, Vance?" she asked, her voice flat, devoid of its usual biting edge.

He took a hesitant step towards her, his eyes searching hers. "Elsa, I'm worried about you. The Butcher's case is taking its toll. You're…changing."

She scoffed, pushing the file away. "Don't be ridiculous, Vance. I'm just doing my job."

"No, Elsa. You're not doing your job. You're becoming what you hunt," he said, his voice gaining a sliver of strength. "You're blurring the lines, Elsa. You're losing yourself."

She stood up, her movements stiff and jerky. "You don't know me, Vance. You don't know what it's like to walk in these shadows, to see the darkness in people's souls. You wouldn't understand."

He stepped closer, his eyes searching hers. "I know you, Elsa. I see the monster you're becoming. And I won't let you lose yourself."

Elsa laughed, a hollow, mirthless sound. "Lose myself? Vance, I haven't lost myself. I've found my true self. I've found my power."

He sighed, his gaze filled with a mixture of fear and sorrow. "Elsa, please. You need to stop this. You need to come back from the edge."

She shook her head, a dark glint in her eyes. "I'm not coming back, Vance. I'm going forward. Into the darkness."

The rain pounded against the window, a steady rhythm of her own internal chaos. Dr. Vance's words, his concern, faded away as Elsa embraced the swirling maelstrom within her. The monster had been awakened. And the hunter had become the hunted.

The Psychiatrists Dilemma

The psychiatrist, Dr. Samuel Hawthorne, watched Elsa Gardner through the one-way mirror, his face a mask of professional neutrality. But inside, his mind churned with a storm of conflicting emotions. He had spent months observing Elsa, the young woman who walked a tightrope between sanity and a chilling, undeniable darkness. He had seen her rise from the ashes of a traumatic childhood, honing her skills and her twisted sense of justice, becoming a

weapon against the very evil that had haunted her. Yet, in recent months, he had witnessed a disturbing shift. Elsa's facade of control was crumbling, the darkness within her creeping to the surface, threatening to consume her entirely.

The case of Elsa Gardner had become a personal obsession for Dr. Hawthorne. He felt an unsettling pull towards this woman, a morbid fascination with her inner world. He yearned to understand her, to delve into the depths of her psyche and grasp the origins of her monstrous desires. He saw in her a reflection of his own inner demons, a testament to the human capacity for both great good and unimaginable evil. He was drawn to her as a moth to a flame, but he knew he had to maintain his professional distance.

He reminded himself of his oath, his duty to protect his patients, even from themselves. But Elsa was a different kind of patient. Her darkness was not a symptom of a disease to be cured, but a fundamental part of her being. Her actions, while horrifying, were driven by a twisted sense of logic, a belief that her victims were somehow deserving of their fates.

The ethical lines blurred. How could he help a woman who

refused to be helped? How could he restrain her darkness when it was intertwined with the very fiber of her being? His own internal battle raged, the conflict between his duty to help and his understanding of her darkness a constant torment.

Elsa, as if sensing his gaze, turned her head, her eyes meeting his through the glass. Her gaze was a chilling blend of amusement and malice, as if she knew exactly what was swirling within him. Dr. Hawthorne felt a shiver run down his spine, a prickling sense of unease. It was as if she had seen into his soul, into the hidden recesses of his mind where his own demons lurked.

"Dr. Hawthorne," she said, her voice a silky whisper that seemed to carry across the distance, "I can see you watching me. Don't you think it's time we had a proper conversation? It's getting rather boring, just observing me through a glass."

Her words, laced with a hint of playful menace, sent a chill through Dr. Hawthorne. He knew he had to maintain control, to stay detached, but the pull towards her, towards the darkness that resided in both their souls, was overwhelming.

"Elsa," he replied, his voice betraying a tremor of fear, "we've discussed this before. These sessions are for your benefit, to help you understand and control..."

"Control?" Elsa laughed, a low, guttural sound that echoed through the room. "Why would I want to control it? It's the only thing that feels real, Dr. Hawthorne. It's the only thing that makes me feel alive."

Her words echoed in Dr. Hawthorne's mind, a chilling reminder of the chasm that separated them. He was a man of reason, a man who sought to heal and understand. She was a woman who embraced her darkness, who revelled in the

power she wielded over life and death.

The more he observed her, the more he realized that she was playing a dangerous game, a game of manipulation. She had become his mirror, reflecting back the darkness that he had always tried to suppress. She challenged him to confront the darkness within himself, to acknowledge the monsters that resided within the human soul.

Elsa's eyes, locked on his through the mirror, held a glint of triumph. She knew that she had him wrapped around her finger, that she had cracked his facade of professional detachment. She was a predator, and he was her prey, caught in the web of her twisted mind.

Dr. Hawthorne knew he couldn't allow this to continue. He needed to take a more active role, to find a way to break through her defenses, to help her before the darkness consumed her completely. But the danger was real, and he was acutely aware that by stepping into the fray, he was potentially putting himself in harm's way.

The battle between his intellect and his instincts raged within him. He knew the risks, but he also knew that he couldn't stand by and watch as Elsa spiraled into a abyss of her own making. He had to find a way to save her, even if it meant facing his own deepest fears.

The psychiatrist's dilemma was far from resolved. He was now caught in a game of psychological chess with Elsa, a battle of wills that could have devastating consequences for both of them. But he couldn't let his fear paralyze him. He had to find a way to confront her darkness, to hold up a mirror to her soul, to see if there was a flicker of humanity, a glimmer of redemption, beneath the monstrous facade she had crafted.

The Game of Manipulation

The air hung heavy in the sterile
confines of the
psychiatrist's office. Elsa, her
sharp eyes locked on Dr.
Thorne's face, traced the lines of his
worried brow, the flicker of
discomfort in his gaze. He was a
master of his craft, trained to dissect
the human psyche, yet Elsa saw
something beyond the professional
detachment. He was playing a
game, a dangerous one, trying to

understand the monster he had created. And she, the monster, was playing along, savoring the thrill of turning the tables.

"You see, Doctor," she began, her voice a silken whisper, "you're afraid of me. Not of my past, not of my actions. But of what I represent. The darkness that exists in all of us, the primal urge to break free from the chains of societal constraints." She leaned forward, her eyes glittering with a cold, calculating gleam. "You're afraid of what I could be, of the potential for chaos I hold."

Dr. Thorne cleared his throat, his gaze avoiding hers. "Elsa," he began cautiously, "I'm not afraid of you. I'm concerned.

Your actions are... extreme. You
need to understand the gravity
of your choices."

"Choices? Doctor," she scoffed, a
sardonic smile playing on her lips.
"You think I have a choice? The
darkness has
always been a part of me, a constant
companion. It
whispered to me in the shadows, lured
me to the precipice of destruction. But
I embraced it, learned to control it. I
am what I am, and you can't change
that."

She rose from the chair, her
movements fluid and graceful, a
predator sizing up its prey. "You see,
Doctor," she continued,

her voice a hypnotic murmur, "you think you're the one pulling the strings. You think you can understand me, dissect me like some lab rat. But I'm a puzzle, a complex one, and you're just a pawn in my game."

Dr. Thorne, his face etched with a mixture of fear and fascination, struggled to maintain his composure. "Elsa," he whispered, his voice strained, "I need you to be honest with me. Why do you do this? Why do you kill?"

"You want the truth, Doctor?" she leaned closer, her breath warm against his face, her eyes burning into his soul. "I kill because it's exhilarating. I kill because it gives me a sense of power, a sense of control. I kill because I can, because no one can stop me. And I kill because it's a reflection of the world around me, a twisted mirror of the injustices, the depravity, the darkness that festers in every corner of this city."

She paused, allowing the words to hang in the air, to burrow into his mind, to sow seeds of doubt and fear. "But I also kill," she continued, her voice dropping to a near whisper, "because I'm a monster, Doctor. A monster that lives within the confines of your own twisted mind. A monster that you fear, that you try to deny, but that you can't escape."

She turned and walked towards the door, her steps confident and deliberate. "I'm not afraid of you,

Doctor," she said over her shoulder, a sly grin playing on her lips. "But you should be afraid of me. Because I'm the one who's in control. And I've only just begun to play the game."

Dr. Thorne watched her leave, his mind reeling. He knew, deep down, that she was right. Elsa was a dangerous game, a force of nature that he could not contain. He had created a monster, a reflection of the darkness that lurked within him, a monster that now threatened to consume him. And he was

powerless to stop it.

Days turned into nights, and the game continued. Elsa, a master manipulator, teased Dr. Thorne, pushed his boundaries, explored the depths of his sanity. She spoke of her past, of the trauma that had shaped her, but her words were carefully crafted, designed to confuse, to mislead. She revealed glimpses of her inner turmoil, her guilt, her struggle for control, but always with a hint of self-satisfaction, a dark humor that sent shivers down his spine.

She was a puzzle, a mystery, and Dr. Thorne was obsessed with finding the solution. But with each session, the lines blurred, the boundaries shifted. He found himself drawn to her, fascinated by her darkness, her raw, unfiltered power. He saw himself in

her, the darkness he had spent a
lifetime suppressing.

One night, late, as the city outside
slept, Dr. Thorne found himself
sitting alone in his office, his
thoughts consumed by Elsa. He had
been examining her file, poring over
her
psychological reports, seeking
answers, but he only found more
questions. The more he learned about
her, the less he understood.

His gaze fell upon a photograph, a
faded image of Elsa as a young girl,
her eyes innocent, her smile wide.
He saw a reflection of himself in her,
a reminder of the innocence he had
lost, the darkness he had buried deep

within.

Suddenly, a chill ran down his spine. He felt a presence in the room, a chilling sensation that sent a shiver through his bones. He turned, his heart pounding, his mind racing.

The office door creaked open, and a figure emerged from the shadows. Elsa, her eyes glittering in the dim light, her smile both captivating and terrifying.

"You see, Doctor," she whispered, her voice soft but deadly, "the game is about to begin."

Dr. Thorne stared at her, his mind reeling. He knew, deep down, that he had made a terrible mistake. He had opened Pandora's Box, and now he was trapped within, at the mercy of the monster he had created. The game was on, and he was no longer the player, but the pawn.

The Whisper of Doubt

The psychiatrist, Dr. James Ashton, had spent countless hours with Elsa, delving into the labyrinthine corridors of her psyche. He had seen the chilling truth behind her calculated facade, witnessed the monstrous desires that lurked beneath her seemingly controlled surface. But now, as he sat across from her, a subtle shift had occurred, a tremor in the foundations of his own perception.

Elsa's words had always been a delicate dance, weaving a tapestry of truth and deception, a carefully crafted performance designed to both seduce and manipulate. He had learned to navigate her words, to decipher the hidden layers of meaning beneath her chillingly calm exterior. But something felt different this time, a subtle shift in the rhythm of her voice, an unnerving familiarity in her gaze.

"Doctor," she began, her voice a silky whisper that sent a shiver down his spine, "don't you ever wonder what lies behind the masks we wear?"

Ashton felt a knot of apprehension tighten in his stomach. He knew she was playing a dangerous game, pushing the boundaries of his sanity, chipping away at the carefully constructed walls of his professional detachment.

"Elsa," he responded, his voice carefully measured, "I understand your anxieties. But we need to focus on your progress, on navigating the path to a healthier state of mind."

"Progress," she scoffed, a sardonic smile playing on her lips.
"A curious word, doctor. It implies a movement towards something better, something more desirable. But what if the

path we're on is the only one we were ever meant to walk?"

Ashton felt a cold wave of unease wash over him. He had seen the darkness that resided within Elsa, the chillingly calculated nature of her actions. But the way she framed her words, the sly, almost seductive implication behind them, was unsettlingly effective. It was as if she was trying to convince him, not of the justification of her crimes, but of the inherent nature of her being, the undeniable truth of her darkness.

"Elsa, I know you've been through a lot, but we need to address your actions, the violence you've inflicted..."

"Violence?" she interrupted, her eyes gleaming with a cold intensity. "Doctor, don't you ever wonder if the world needs a little more balance? A little less of the saccharine sweetness of the good, a little more of the raw, uncompromising truth of the darkness?"

He saw her point, the stark reality of the world's horrors, the countless acts of cruelty that went unpunished. But he knew the danger of her logic, the seductive allure of the darkness she championed.

"What you're saying, Elsa, is dangerous. It's a slippery slope, a justification for the very things we strive to prevent."

"But Doctor," she countered, her voice taking on a seductive whisper, "who is to say what's right and wrong? Who gets to decide the rules of this twisted game?"

Ashton felt a surge of anger, a desperate need to maintain his composure. He had to be the one to hold onto the thread of reason in this chaotic dance, to resist the insidious pull of her words.

"Elsa, you need to understand that your actions have consequences. You can't escape the reality of the harm you've caused."

"Consequences," she murmured, leaning back in her chair, a hint of a knowing smile playing on her lips. "Tell me, Doctor, have you ever truly understood the nature of consequences? The way they can be both devastating and strangely liberating?"

He felt his heart racing, a sense of dread settling over him. He had never seen her like this, so openly challenging his beliefs, his very perception of reality.

"Elsa," he pleaded, his voice strained, "We need to talk about your past, about the path that led you here."

She let out a low, melodic laugh, her eyes holding a chilling intensity that sent a tremor through him.

"Doctor, do you think the past has any real power? Or is it just a story we tell ourselves, a narrative we use to justify our present actions?"

Ashton felt a cold sweat breaking out on his forehead. He was losing his grip, the familiar ground beneath his feet shifting into a treacherous abyss of doubt. He knew she was playing a dangerous game, but he couldn't seem to break free from the hypnotic pull of her words.

"Elsa, I'm here to help you. We can work through this together..."

"Help?" she scoffed, her voice dripping with disdain.

"Doctor, do you think I need your help? I'm not broken. I'm simply different, a creature of a different world, a world where the rules are written in blood and the darkness is not

something to be feared, but embraced."

Ashton found himself speechless, his mind struggling to process the torrent of unsettling thoughts swirling within him. Her words had planted seeds of doubt, a whisper of uncertainty that threatened to unravel the very foundation of his beliefs. He had always believed in the power of reason, in the ability to understand

and dissect the human psyche. But in Elsa's presence, he felt the fragility of his convictions, the terrifying possibility that she might be right, that the line between sanity and insanity was far more porous than he had ever imagined.

He watched her as she rose from her chair, her gaze unwavering, her presence radiating an aura of confident power. It was as if she had seen into the depths of his soul, exposed the hidden doubts that had always lurked beneath the surface of his carefully constructed facade.

"Thank you for the session, Doctor," she said, her voice a chillingly calm whisper. "I think I'll be needing a new therapist soon. Someone who can truly understand the nature of the darkness."

He watched as she walked away, her silhouette a haunting figure against the stark white walls of his office. He felt a shiver run down his spine, the chilling realization that he had been outmaneuvered, his mind a battleground of unsettling doubts. He had always prided himself on his ability to control his emotions, to maintain a detached objectivity. But Elsa had pierced through his defenses, exposing the vulnerabilities beneath, the seeds of uncertainty she had so deftly planted.

He knew he needed to regain control, to reclaim his sense of balance. But the whispers of doubt remained, a lingering echo in the depths of his mind, a haunting reminder of the

unsettling encounter with the woman who walked a razor-thin line between sanity and the abyss. He knew he had to find a way to resist the insidious pull of her darkness, to restore the equilibrium he had so carefully crafted. But as he sank back into his chair, the chilling possibility remained, a cold and unsettling truth: he was no longer sure he could distinguish between the hunter and the hunted.

The Turning Point

The air in Dr. Vance's office hung heavy with the weight of unspoken truths. Elsa's gaze, cool and calculating, met his across the polished mahogany desk. The sterile white walls felt like a prison, a stark contrast to the intricate tapestry of her own twisted mind. Each session with the psychiatrist was a dance of veiled truths, a psychological chess game where the stakes were their sanity.

Dr. Vance had seen countless souls fractured by trauma, minds warped by darkness, but Elsa was a different breed. A predator who embraced her own savagery, her desire for justice twisted into a morbid hunger for retribution. She was a walking contradiction, a creature both captivating and terrifying.

He had tried to understand her, to unravel the threads of her past that led her down this perilous path. But with each session, he found himself sinking deeper into the murky depths of her psyche, questioning his own objectivity, his own ability to remain an impartial observer.

He recalled the chilling scene from their last session, her words echoing in his mind like a haunting melody. "Do you truly believe in justice, Dr. Vance? Or are you just another sheep in a world of blind obedience?" The question, posed with a deceptively

calm voice, had shaken him to his
core.
He knew she was playing a
game, pushing his buttons,
testing his limits.

Elsa was a master manipulator, her charm a
lethal weapon.
She had a way of weaving words
into seductive traps,
leading him down a labyrinth of
doubt and self-questioning.

The line between patient
and predator had become
increasingly blurred.

He had always prided himself on his objectivity, on his ability to maintain a clinical detachment, to separate his emotions from his duty. But with Elsa, that detachment seemed to be crumbling, replaced by a dangerous fascination, a terrifying curiosity about the abyss that resided within her.

He knew she was a threat, a danger to herself and to anyone who crossed her path. Yet, he found himself strangely drawn to her, fascinated by the darkness that pulsed within her, the undeniable power she exuded. It was as if her shadow, a creature born of pain and rage, had wrapped itself around him, whispering temptations into his ear.

He couldn't deny the truth anymore. He was no longer just a detached observer. Elsa had somehow infiltrated his thoughts, her presence a constant hum in his mind, a voice whispering in the back of his consciousness. The question that haunted him now was no longer about her sanity, but his own. Could he stay objective, remain a detached professional, when his own sanity was under threat?

He found himself looking at her with a mixture of fear and fascination. Elsa, the predator, was no longer just a case. She had become a reflection, a horrifying mirror reflecting the darkness that lurked within him.

He was no longer sure if he was helping her or merely feeding the fire that raged within her. He was caught in a dangerous game, a game he might not win, a game where the stakes were his own soul.

"Elsa," he finally spoke, his voice a mere whisper, "I think…I think we need to take a different approach."

Elsa raised a single eyebrow, her expression a mixture of amusement and challenge. "A different approach, Dr. Vance? You mean a more…active one?"

He knew then that he had crossed the line. He had become entangled, ensnared by the web she had so meticulously woven. But the truth was, he couldn't help himself. He had to know, he had to understand, even if it meant risking everything.

"Yes," he said, his voice trembling slightly, "Something more…involving."

He knew the danger, knew the potential for self-destruction, but he couldn't turn back. He had become entangled with Elsa, and there was no escape. He had to find a way to stop her, to pull her back from the abyss, even if it meant risking his own sanity, even if it meant becoming the very thing he feared.

The game was on, and they were both playing for keeps.

The next few weeks were a whirlwind of both exhilarating and terrifying moments. Dr. Vance, spurred by a desperate need to understand and possibly control Elsa, began to delve deeper into her world, venturing into the dangerous territories she haunted. He shadowed her, a silent observer, watching as she navigated the dark underbelly of society, a world of shadows and secrets where the lines between right and wrong blurred, where the seductive allure of darkness held a chilling power.

He discovered that she had a remarkable ability to blend in, to become invisible in the shadows, a chameleon shifting colors with every move. He watched as she manipulated people, using their own vulnerabilities and desires against

them, a puppet master pulling strings in the shadows.

As he followed her, he found himself experiencing a disturbing mix of emotions. He was simultaneously terrified of her, mesmerized by her, and horrified by the depths of her darkness. Yet, he was unable to turn away, compelled by a dark fascination that he couldn't quite explain.

He knew that he was walking a thin line, a line that could easily snap, plunging him into the abyss. He understood the danger, but he couldn't help himself. He was drawn to her, drawn to the power she wielded, to the twisted logic that justified her actions.

One night, he found himself outside a dingy bar, a place known for its shady clientele and the whispers of forbidden desires. Elsa was inside, a predator lurking in the shadows, her gaze searching for her next victim. Dr. Vance, hidden in the darkness, watched as she approached a man, her smile a mesmerizing trap, a weapon that lured unsuspecting prey.

The man, a middle-aged businessman, was captivated by her charm, unaware of the darkness that lurked beneath the surface. She was already weaving her spell, using his vulnerabilities against him, manipulating his desires, leading him down a path of self-destruction.

Dr. Vance knew that he should intervene, that he should call the authorities. But something held him back, a morbid curiosity, a desire to see how far Elsa would go, how deep her descent into darkness would be.

He watched as she led the man deeper into the bar, a chilling dance of seduction and manipulation. His heart pounded in his chest, a mixture of fear and anticipation.

He knew that he was losing his grip on reality, that he was

becoming entangled in Elsa's twisted web, but he couldn't stop.

As he watched the scene unfold, a strange sense of exhilaration coursed through him. The line between observer and participant, between doctor and patient, had blurred, a dangerous dance on the edge of a precipice.

The bar, once a sanctuary of forbidden desires, became a stage for a dangerous psychological battle.

And Dr. Vance, the supposed savior, was an unwilling participant in a game that could destroy them both.

The Confrontation of Minds

The air in the sterile white room was thick with unspoken tension, the only sound the rhythmic ticking of the clock on the wall. Elsa, her back ramrod straight in the leather armchair, stared out the window at the cityscape, her gaze distant, her thoughts a labyrinth of darkness. Dr. Samuel Vance, his face etched with concern and a hint of weary fascination, watched her, his eyes probing, seeking a glimpse into the depths of her soul.

Their sessions had become a twisted dance, a psychological game of cat and mouse played in the confines of a psychiatrist's office. Elsa, with her unsettlingly calm demeanor and the glint of steel in her eyes, was a puzzle Vance found himself both captivated and terrified by. He knew she was a killer, her past crimes a grim testament to the darkness that resided within her, yet she wore it like a second skin, seemingly impervious to the weight of her deeds.

Vance, a seasoned professional, was used to dealing with troubled minds, but Elsa was unlike anything he had encountered before. She was a paradox, a woman who reveled in the thrill of the hunt, who saw herself as a righteous avenger, while simultaneously embracing the seductive allure of her own destructive impulses. He had tried to delve into her psyche, to understand the roots of her violence, but Elsa, with her guarded demeanor and carefully constructed facade, remained an enigma.

Today, Vance was determined to break through her defenses. He cleared his throat, his voice measured, "Elsa, I need you to be honest with me. You've shown remarkable restraint in your… actions. But there's a darkness inside you, a hunger

for violence that you haven't fully addressed. What's driving you? What compels you to kill?"

Elsa turned her head, her eyes meeting his with a chilling intensity that made Vance's spine tingle. "I kill because I have to," she said, her voice a low, measured tone. "Because the world is full of monsters, and someone has to make it right."

"And how do you define 'right', Elsa?" Vance pressed, his tone unwavering. "Is it right to take a life, even if it's a life that has caused harm?"

"It's not about right or wrong," Elsa countered, her gaze fixed on him. "It's about balance. The world is a delicate ecosystem, and when it's out of balance, someone has to restore it."

"And you're the one who gets to decide who needs restoring?" Vance countered, leaning forward, his voice tinged with a sense of urgency. "Who gives you the right to play God, Elsa?"

Elsa chuckled, a dry, brittle sound that sent shivers down Vance's spine. "God plays dice with the universe," she said, her voice low and deliberate. "I play with the monsters."

The silence in the room stretched, thick with unspoken truths and the weight of their respective convictions. Vance, his heart pounding in his chest, felt a wave of unease wash over him. He had never encountered a patient who so readily embraced their own darkness, who seemed to revel in the power they wielded over life and death. It was a dangerous game, and Elsa, it seemed, was a master player.

"Elsa," he began, his voice measured. "You have a unique perspective on the world. You see things most people don't,

and your skills… your abilities… they're extraordinary. But you need to understand, this path you've chosen, it's not sustainable."

"I'm not afraid of what I am," Elsa said, her gaze unwavering. "I'm not afraid of the darkness."

"But you should be," Vance said, his voice firm. "The darkness can consume you,

Elsa. It already has."

Elsa remained silent, her expression
unreadable, her thoughts shrouded in
a veil of shadows. Vance, his mind
racing,
realized he was fighting a losing
battle. He was facing a woman who
was not only a killer but a master of
manipulation, a predator who saw his
attempts to reach her as a mere game,
an obstacle to overcome.

He had to tread carefully, he knew,
for to antagonize her further could be
disastrous. He decided to change
tactics, to try and appeal to the
remnants of empathy he believed
still lurked within her.

"Elsa," he said, his voice softened. "I understand you're angry. You've experienced pain and betrayal, and you're seeking justice. But there are other ways to find that justice, ways that don't involve taking a life."

Elsa snorted, her disdain palpable. "Justice isn't served through legal processes," she said, her voice laced with bitterness. "It's served through retribution."

Vance sighed, feeling a sense of frustration welling up inside him. He had hoped to find a flicker of doubt in her eyes, a crack in her armor. But Elsa, it seemed, was impervious to reason, convinced of the righteousness of her own twisted morality.

He decided to shift gears once more, to try and expose the vulnerability he sensed beneath her icy exterior.

"Elsa," he said, his voice gentle. "You're not the only one who has experienced pain. You're not the only one who has been hurt."

Elsa's eyes narrowed, her gaze piercing. "Don't try to play the pity card, Vance," she said, her voice laced with warning.
"I don't need your sympathy."

"I'm not offering sympathy," Vance countered, his voice unwavering. "I'm offering you a chance to heal. You've carried this burden for too long, Elsa. It's time to let it go."

Elsa stood abruptly, her chair scraping across the floor, the sound jarring in the otherwise silent room. She turned towards him, her face a mask of icy indifference.

"I'm not here for healing, Vance," she said, her voice cold and sharp. "I'm here for a purpose. I'm here to kill the monsters."

With those words, she turned and left, leaving Vance alone in the silent office, the weight of her words settling upon him like a shroud. He knew he was facing a formidable adversary, a woman who was not only a killer but a walking embodiment of darkness. He had to find a way to reach her, to understand her, to prevent her from consuming herself in her own twisted sense of justice. But the clock was ticking, and the darkness within Elsa seemed to grow with each passing moment.

The Final Chase

The city was a labyrinth of shadows, a concrete jungle teeming with secrets and the stench of decay. Elsa, her senses sharpened by years of training and a twisted sense of justice, stalked through its dark alleys and forgotten corners. Her prey, a new serial killer who left behind a trail of blood and macabre artistry, was a ghost in the urban wilderness.

Each clue she found was a piece of a puzzle, a cryptic message in the city's morbid tapestry. Torn photographs, a single crimson rose left on a victim's chest, a cryptic message scrawled on a graffiti-covered wall - the killer was playing a game, and Elsa, the hunter, was forced to play along.

The city felt like a living, breathing entity, its secrets

whispered in the wind, its shadows concealing the killer's next move. She followed the scent of fear, the cold trail of a predator who reveled in the darkness he created.

Her instincts, honed by years of tracking down the worst humanity had to offer, whispered of a pattern, a rhyme and reason behind the seemingly random killings. The victims, all young women, were connected by an invisible thread, their lives intertwined in a way that eluded even the most astute detective.

Elsa, however, saw the thread, the twisted logic behind the killer's actions. He was a puppeteer, pulling the strings of his victims, a twisted artist crafting his masterpiece in blood.

She wasn't chasing a monster, not in the traditional sense.

She was chasing a reflection of herself, a darker, more primal version of her own twisted sense of justice.

She had become the city's guardian, the protector against the nightmarish creatures that crawled in its underbelly. She was the wolf in sheep's clothing, a predator forced to become the hunter, a twisted reflection of the darkness she hunted.

As the chase intensified, she felt a strange kinship with the killer, a disturbing echo of her own darkness resonating in his actions. He was a mirror, reflecting back the demons she fought so hard to suppress. The city, a canvas for his twisted artistry, became the stage for a battle between two predators, a deadly game of cat and mouse played out against the backdrop of urban decay.

Elsa, her mind a kaleidoscope of memories and the chilling whispers of her past, was losing herself in the chase. The city, with its dark underbelly, its secrets and whispers, was becoming her own personal purgatory.

The hunt was a journey into the heart of darkness, a descent into a world where the line between hunter and hunted blurred, where the predator and the prey danced a deadly waltz. She was chasing the killer, but she was also chasing a reflection of herself, a dark truth hidden beneath the facade of her own sanity.

Days blurred into nights, each encounter with the killer a chilling dance with death. The city, once a familiar
backdrop, was transformed into a sinister labyrinth, its
secrets seeping into her mind, whispering promises of danger and the seductive allure of darkness.

The climax was inevitable, a confrontation born from the shadows of a city that had become a vessel for the killer's twisted desires. The battle would be one of wits and instinct, of predator against predator, a clash of two souls intertwined by the threads of darkness.

And in the heart of that confrontation, Elsa would be forced to confront the monster within, the darkness that resided in her soul, the chilling truth that she was, in many ways, a reflection of the very evil she hunted.

The Twisted Games

The city of blood pulsed with an unsettling rhythm, its neon signs a grotesque mockery of the darkness that bled into the concrete canyons. Rain lashed against the grimy windows of the abandoned warehouse, each drop a miniature echo of the violence that simmered beneath the surface. Elsa Gardner, her senses heightened by the adrenaline coursing through her veins, crouched in the shadows, her breath a ragged whisper against the humid air.

She had been on the killer's trail for weeks, tracing his twisted game through the labyrinthine underbelly of the city.

Each clue, a cryptic message, a gruesome tableau, pushed her closer to the heart of the darkness. The killer, a master of manipulation, reveled in the hunt, taunting Elsa with his intellect, leaving her to decipher his twisted logic, to navigate the maze of his mind.

He was a mirror to her own darkness, a reflection of the monster she had wrestled with since childhood. His victims, chosen with meticulous care, were echoes of her own past, reminders of the horrors she had buried deep within. Each kill, a macabre performance, a grotesque dance orchestrated to provoke her, to unravel the fragile threads of her control.

He had led her to this abandoned warehouse, a decaying monument to the city's forgotten nightmares. The air hung heavy with the stench of decay, the silence punctuated by the rhythmic drip of water, a metronome marking the passage of time. This was his stage, his final act, and Elsa, the reluctant audience, was about to take center stage.

She moved with a predatory grace, honed by years of

training, a silent shadow against the decaying walls. Her senses were sharpened, her every move calculated, a testament to the years she had spent perfecting the art of the hunt. But this was a different kind of prey, a creature of her own making, a reflection of the darkness she had chosen to embrace.

A low growl rumbled in her throat, a primal instinct
awakened by the scent of blood, the thrill of the hunt. He was playing with her, testing her limits, and she, in turn, was enjoying the game. A dangerous game, where the stakes were higher than ever before, where the lines between
predator and prey were blurred beyond recognition.

A flicker of movement caught her eye, a shadow shifting in the corner of her vision. She froze, her muscles taut, her senses screaming with anticipation. A faint metallic tang lingered in the air, the scent of blood, a beacon in the darkness. She had him, he was within reach, the final act was about to begin.

The killer, a man shrouded in darkness, materialized from the shadows, his eyes gleaming with a feral intensity. He stood tall, a silhouette against the flickering lights, an image of confidence, of control. His smile, a twisted mockery of human kindness, stretched across his face, revealing a chilling glint in his eyes.

"So, the huntress has finally found her prey," he drawled, his voice a low, hypnotic murmur. "I must say, you've surprised me, Ms. Gardner. You're more tenacious than I expected." He took a step forward, his movements fluid, predatory.

Elsa stood her ground, her gaze unwavering, her hand hovering near the hilt of her concealed blade. "The game is almost over," she countered, her voice a cold whisper. "And the predator will finally meet his end."

Their eyes locked in a silent battle of wills, a contest of power, of darkness. The air crackled with tension, the anticipation thick enough to choke on. The final dance had begun, a deadly choreography of predator and prey, a battle for survival and the fate of their souls.

He moved again, his movements a fluid blur, a calculated attack. He lunged for her, his hand reaching for her throat, his eyes burning with a lust for dominance. Elsa reacted instinctively, her hand flashing, her blade singing through the air. He stumbled back, his hand clutched to his chest, the blade glinting where it had pierced his flesh.

He hissed, a guttural sound of pain and anger, his eyes narrowing into slits. "You think you can stop me, Ms. Gardner?" He snarled, his voice a guttural growl. "I've been waiting for this moment, for years. I've been playing this game, and you're just another pawn."

Elsa laughed, a chilling, mirthless sound that echoed in the silence. "You think you've won, but you've only played into my hand." She stepped closer, her gaze cold, her resolve hardened. "You are a mere reflection of my own darkness, and I will not allow you to corrupt me any further."

He lurched forward, his movements fueled by rage and desperation. He was a wounded animal, cornered and desperate, but Elsa was ready for him. She danced back, her movements precise, her blade a deadly extension of her will.

Each parry, each thrust, was a dance of death, a deadly ballet of skill and instinct. He was fast, unpredictable, but Elsa was quicker, more ruthless. The warehouse floor became their arena, the air thick with the scent of blood and desperation.

He slashed, he lunged, he roared, but she remained a blur, a

phantom, a shadow, always one step ahead. She moved with the precision of a surgeon, her blade slicing through the air, her eyes gleaming with a cold, calculating fury.

He was a mirror, a reflection of her own darkness, but she was the hunter, and he was the prey. And she would not falter, she would not fail. She would finish the game, she would bring the darkness to an end.

The final confrontation was swift, brutal, a symphony of violence orchestrated to a deadly tempo. He had backed himself into a corner, his movements slow, his energy depleted. Elsa stood before him, her blade poised, her face a mask of cold resolve.

She moved, her blade a lightning strike, a symphony of steel and flesh.

He staggered back, a gurgling sound escaping his lips, his eyes wide with disbelief. He slumped to the floor, his body a canvas of crimson, a testament to the darkness that had consumed him.

Elsa stood over him, her breathing ragged, her body trembling with the aftermath of the fight. She sheathed her blade, her eyes fixed on the broken man at her feet. He was no longer a threat, he was nothing but a broken shell, a reminder of the darkness that had consumed him.

She turned and walked away, leaving him to the silence of the decaying warehouse, a final act in the bloody play that was her life.

The city of blood swallowed her up, the darkness claiming her as its own.

But she was no longer just a hunter, she was something more. She was the reflection of the darkness, the embodiment of the violence she had embraced. And she knew, with a chilling certainty, that the game had just begun.

The Unmasking

The city was a tapestry of shadows and secrets, its

labyrinthine alleys and flickering streetlights casting an eerie glow on the night. Elsa, her senses honed by years of

training and a lifetime of darkness, moved like a ghost

through the urban underbelly, her gaze fixed on the trail of the killer she hunted. Every rustle of wind, every distant echo, was a potential clue, a whisper of the monster she sought.

The chase had been relentless, a game of cat and mouse played out in the heart of a city steeped in blood. The killer, a master puppeteer, had left a trail of carefully orchestrated acts, each one a morbid masterpiece designed to taunt and torment. Elsa, fueled by a burning need to stop him, found herself drawn into his twisted game, a dark dance of predator and prey.

As she followed the breadcrumbs of his twisted path, Elsa felt a growing sense of unease. The killer's MO, his meticulous planning and calculated brutality, echoed a haunting familiarity within her own psyche. It was a

disturbing realization, one that sent a shiver down her spine, a whisper of doubt creeping into her mind. Was she hunting a reflection of herself, a monster born from the same darkness that resided within her?

The city, a silent witness to countless crimes, seemed to hum with a sinister energy, a palpable sense of dread that clung to the air like a shroud. The faces of the city, obscured by the flickering shadows, became a blur, their eyes reflecting the same fear and uncertainty that gnawed at Elsa's core. Every corner she turned, every street she traversed, was a potential

trap, a reminder of the constant danger that lurked in the shadows.

The trail led her to a dilapidated warehouse on the city's edge, a place where shadows danced and whispers seemed to coil around the corners. It was a place where the city's heart beat with a dark, pulsating rhythm, a haven for the lost and the damned. As she approached, Elsa could feel her heart pounding in her chest, the adrenaline coursing through her veins, a potent cocktail of fear and anticipation.

Inside the warehouse, the air hung heavy with the stench of decay and the whispers of forgotten stories. The floor was littered with debris, a testament to years of neglect and decay. Elsa's senses were on high alert, her eyes scanning every inch of the space, searching for any sign of the killer.
She moved with purpose, each step calculated, her mind racing with possibilities.

The killer, she knew, had been using this warehouse as a staging ground, a place to plan his macabre performances. Every inch of the place

was a potential clue, a testament to his twisted mind. Elsa, armed with her knowledge of
forensics and her honed instincts, began to piece together the puzzle, searching for the missing pieces that would reveal his identity.

In the dim light, Elsa noticed a faint scent, a subtle trace of a chemical she recognized from her training. It was a chemical used in a specific type of anesthetic, one that left no trace in the system, a common tool for those who practiced a certain type of deadly art.

It was a chilling realization. The killer was a professional, someone who knew how to cover his tracks, someone who was not afraid to leave a trail of destruction in his wake. The scent, a lingering whisper of his presence, ignited a surge of

adrenaline within Elsa. She was close, closer than she had ever been, and the stakes were higher than ever.

With renewed determination, Elsa continued her search, her focus laser-sharp. She examined every nook and cranny, every piece of debris, searching for any sign that could lead her to the killer. Time was running out, and she knew that every moment wasted could mean another innocent life lost.

Finally, in the dim light of a dusty corner, she saw it. A single, seemingly insignificant detail, but one that sent a jolt of recognition through her. It was a small, faded inscription on the side of a metal box, barely visible beneath layers of grime and dust.

The inscription, barely legible, read: "The Raven's Nest."

A name, a seemingly innocuous phrase, but one that sent a cold shiver down Elsa's spine. It was a name that held a terrifying significance, a name that was deeply etched in the darkest recesses of her memory. The Raven's Nest, a place of unimaginable horrors, a place where she had once been a victim, a place where she had

witnessed the brutal,
unimaginable acts that had fueled her
descent into darkness.

Her past, the memories she had tried
to bury, the horrors she had tried to
forget, were now coming back to
haunt her. The killer, the monster she
hunted, was not just some nameless,
faceless entity. He was someone she
knew, someone she had once feared,
someone who had shaped the darkest
corners of her soul.

It was a horrifying realization, one
that threatened to shatter her fragile
facade, to unravel the carefully crafted
lies she had told herself for so long.
The hunter, the one who pursued
darkness, was now trapped in the
labyrinth of her own past. The city of

blood, with its secrets and shadows, had become

a mirror reflecting her own twisted history.

Elsa felt a surge of primal fear, a deep, instinctive terror that threatened to consume her. Her carefully constructed persona, the mask she wore to hide the darkness within, was beginning to crack, revealing the monster she had tried so desperately to suppress.

The chase had become a personal battle, a twisted game of vengeance and redemption played out against the backdrop of a city steeped in blood. Elsa, the hunter, was now the hunted, forced to confront the demons of her past, the horrors she had inflicted, and the consequences of the path she had chosen.

As she stood in the shadows of the warehouse, the scent of the killer's presence lingering in the air, she knew that the game had changed. This was not just a hunt anymore. This was a journey into the darkest recesses of her own soul, a quest for redemption, a battle for her own sanity. The city of blood, with its secrets and shadows, had become a mirror reflecting her own twisted history. She was no longer just a hunter, she was a reflection of the darkness she sought to destroy.

The Consequence of Choice

The city, a concrete jungle draped in a perpetual twilight, pulsated with the rhythm of chaos. Elsa, a shadow flitting through its labyrinthine streets, felt its heartbeat resonate within her own. She was a predator, a hunter, a weapon meticulously crafted for the dark game that consumed her life. Yet, as she stalked her latest prey, a ghost from the past, the city's suffocating embrace began to feel more like a vice tightening around her soul. The city of blood, as she'd come to think of it, mirrored the battlefield raging within her. Each kill, each victory, had carved a deeper trench in her psyche, a scar she couldn't erase. Her eyes, once blazing with righteous fury, now flickered with a unsettling emptiness. The psychiatrist, a man who tried to map the topography of her darkness, had warned her of this descent. He'd seen the seductive allure of power, the insidious whispers that promised dominion over chaos. And Elsa, driven by a need to control the darkness within, had readily embraced the role of hunter, wielding her skills like a blade against the world's evils.

But tonight, the city pulsed with a different rhythm. It wasn't just the symphony of sirens and the distant screams that vibrated against her senses. It was a new kind of darkness, a chilling echo from her own past, a whisper from a forgotten nightmare.

The killer she hunted wasn't just another
nameless face in the city's vast tapestry of pain. He was a ghost from her own childhood, a twisted reflection of her darkest desires, a stark reminder of the journey she had taken. Each step forward felt like a stumble backward, each pulse of her heart a testament to the fragile line she walked between redemption and self-destruction.

She stalked him through the city's underbelly, a maze of shadows and whispers. Each alley, each crumbling facade, held a silent story of violence and decay. It was a world she'd come

to know intimately, its grim beauty a
perverse comfort.

The chase was exhilarating, a dance
with death where she held the lead.
Yet, as she closed in on her target, the
city's suffocating grip tightened, the
echo of her past a constant reminder
of the consequences of her choices.
The lines blurred, the morality of her
actions a tangled web of twisted logic.
Was she a savior, a protector against
the world's worst monsters, or was she
becoming the very monster she sought
to destroy?

A gnawing doubt, a relentless voice
within, whispered its insidious
message. She couldn't escape the
echoes of her past, the chilling
specters of those she'd wronged. Each
victim, a face etched in her mind, a

reminder of the toll she'd taken. As she cornered her prey, a man who embodied the fear she'd long carried within, the city's pulse thrummed with a sickening beat. It was a heartbeat she could feel in her own chest, a sickening reminder of the darkness that consumed her. She had the power to end his reign, to deliver justice for the city. Yet, in that moment, as his eyes met hers, she saw not just the reflection of her own past, but the potential for her own descent into oblivion.

The choice was stark and unforgiving. Embrace the darkness, become the very monster she hunted, or fight for a sliver of redemption, a chance to escape the city of blood's suffocating embrace.

Her hands, calloused and trained for violence, trembled slightly. She could feel the city's watchful gaze, a silent chorus of anticipation. But beneath the city's facade of chaos, she saw the faint flicker of a different kind of light, a whisper of hope that dared to challenge the abyss. It was a beacon, a flickering ember of humanity, a promise of a different path. The city waited, its silence a deafening roar. And Elsa, caught in the crossfire of her past and the

promise of a future yet unwritten, made a choice that would forever alter the course of her destiny.

The Climax

The city's steel and glass facade, slick and gleaming under the artificial light, felt like a mirror reflecting her own fractured soul. The air was thick with the scent of rain and decay, a potent cocktail that matched the swirling storm in Elsa's gut. The chase had brought her to the heart of the city, a labyrinth of darkness where shadows held secrets and the echo of screams lingered in the alleyways.

She moved with a hunter's grace, her footsteps echoing in the silence of the abandoned warehouse district. The scent of blood, faint but unmistakable, led her through the maze of derelict buildings, each rusting frame a potential hiding place, a whispered promise of the nightmare unfolding within. She was on the trail of a beast, a predator who mirrored her own twisted impulses, a reflection in the dark abyss of her soul.

His methods were chillingly familiar. He relished the power, the control, the cold satisfaction of taking another life. He was an artist of the macabre, leaving behind gruesome trophies of his victims, a twisted testament to his dark obsession. Elsa, driven by a strange mix of repulsion and fascination, couldn't deny the unsettling connection to the killer's handiwork. She knew his dance, his twisted logic, his hunger for the ultimate prize. He was a mirror image of her own darkness, an echo of the monster she'd carefully kept caged.

The flickering neon signs, broken and faded, cast elongated shadows that danced with the wind, creating a phantasmagorical spectacle of death. The city was a stage, and Elsa was caught in the final act of a bloody play, the

script written by her own tormented past. The air felt electric, charged with the anticipation of a showdown that would define the fate of both her life and her soul.

As she crept deeper into the abandoned warehouse, the silence was broken only by the pounding of her own heart, a relentless rhythm matching the escalating danger. She could sense him, a presence in the shadows, a predator in the shadows, patiently waiting for his prey. Each creak of the floorboards, each sigh of the wind, sent shivers down her spine, a constant reminder of the unseen menace lurking in the darkness.

The warehouse, a hulking monument to decay, was a sprawling cavern filled with forgotten machinery and the lingering scent of dust and despair. It was a perfect stage for the final act of this twisted drama, a crucible where shadows danced and fate was decided in the blink of an eye.

A flicker of movement in the dim light caught her eye. The killer, a tall, imposing figure, stepped out of the shadows, his face obscured by the darkness. He was a shadow, a phantom, a creature of the night, his eyes gleaming with an intensity that made Elsa's blood run cold.

"Elsa," he rasped, his voice a chilling whisper that echoed through the warehouse. "I've been waiting for you."

The air thickened with anticipation, the silence heavy with the weight of their shared past, their intertwined destinies. He was the embodiment of her deepest fears, the predator she'd been running from for so long. He was the monster she'd kept hidden, the shadow she'd tried to banish.

He wasn't just a killer, a creature of darkness. He was a piece of her past, a haunting reminder of the trauma that had
shaped her into the monster she'd become. The revelation

sent a jolt of terror through her veins, an instinctive
recognition of the dark truth he represented. She had been running from herself all this time, a chase that had led her to this chilling

confrontation.

"I know who you are," she said, her voice steady despite the storm brewing within. Her words were a confession, a whispered acknowledgment of the dark truths that bound them. The killer, her reflection in the mirror of her own soul, held the key to the secrets that haunted her, the memories she'd tried to bury deep within.

He smiled, a chilling, predatory grin that illuminated his face. It was a smile that mirrored the twisted grin that had been etched into her own subconscious. He had become her dark doppelganger, the twisted reflection of her deepest desires.

"I know you too, Elsa," he said, his voice a seductive whisper, promising both pleasure and pain. "You are more like me than you'd like to believe."

His words pierced her, a chilling truth she couldn't escape. He knew her secrets, her darkest desires, the monster she kept caged within. His recognition was a mirror held up to her own soul, a reflection of her twisted reflection.

The confrontation felt inevitable, as if it had been ordained from the moment she took her first breath. It was a battle for survival, a clash of two predators, a struggle for the dominance of darkness. But it was also a battle for her soul, a final showdown with the monster within.

The warehouse seemed to shrink, the walls closing in, the shadows tightening their grip. Elsa, her senses heightened, prepared for a fight, a dance of death with a creature born from her own darkness.

The air crackled with the anticipation of violence, the scent of blood heavy in the air. She knew this was a dance she couldn't escape, a confrontation that would decide the fate of her soul, a reckoning with the monster she had become. The city of blood, with its

dark heart and labyrinthine alleys, was
a stage for the final act of her twisted
journey, a testament to the power of
darkness and the haunting resilience
of the human spirit.

The Weight of Sacrifice

The sterile white walls of the CIA safe
house felt like a prison, even though it
was meant to be a sanctuary. Elsa
stared out the window, the cityscape a
blur of neon and concrete, each
flickering light a reminder of the
chaos she had wrought. The weight of
her actions pressed down on her, a

suffocating blanket of guilt.

She had just finished her latest assignment, a brutal dance with a killer whose twisted mind echoed her own. He was gone, another soul extinguished, and the satisfaction of the kill, the fleeting sense of justice, was gone, replaced by an emptiness that gnawed at her insides.

Each time she took a life, she told herself it was an act of redemption, a necessary evil to rid the world of its most vile creatures. But as the body count grew, the line between righteous vengeance and cold-blooded murder blurred. The horrors she inflicted on others, the raw terror she witnessed, it all reflected back onto her, twisting her soul into a knot of despair.

Her therapist, Dr. Davies, a man with
eyes that saw through her carefully
constructed facade, had warned her
about this.
He called it the "monster's
mirror," the reflection of the
darkness within staring back at
her with each kill.

She had scoffed at his
pronouncements initially, dismissing
him as a man who could only
understand the shadows of her past
but couldn't grasp the intricacies of
her present, her twisted logic. Yet,
deep within her, a seed of doubt had
taken root, a nagging suspicion that
the price of her actions was far greater

than she had anticipated.

The memories haunted her. The lifeless eyes of the goose she had killed as a child, the cold fear in her college classmate's gaze, the desperate plea in her roommate's voice before she took revenge on her attacker. Each face, each fleeting
moment, echoed in her dreams, a tapestry of guilt woven into the fabric of her psyche.

It was a vicious cycle. The thrill of the kill, the power it bestowed, the fleeting sense of control it offered, all of it was a seductive poison that slowly seeped into her being. Yet, the aftermath, the chilling realization of the life she had taken, the knowledge of the pain she had caused, it left her hollow and desolate.

She looked at her hands, the calloused knuckles, the scars from years of MMA training, the tools of her trade. She had always been fascinated by the mechanisms of life and death, the delicate balance between the two. But now, she saw only the ugliness, the bloodstains that wouldn't wash away.

The world outside the safe house seemed to mock her,
oblivious to the darkness she carried.
People walked by, laughing, talking, their lives a symphony of normalcy, a stark contrast to the symphony of

violence that played out in her mind.

She couldn't escape the weight of her actions, the sacrifices she had made. The line between hunter and hunted had become a blurry, suffocating fog, and she was caught in the middle, her soul a battlefield between the monster she had become and the remnants of the woman she used to be.

Dr. Davies had told her that a monster could only survive by feeding. He had also said that a monster could choose to starve, to fight for a semblance of humanity, however fleeting. But the hunger gnawed at her, a constant reminder of the monster lurking within.

She wasn't sure if she could resist the
temptation forever.
The darkness was a siren song, its
allure intoxicating, its promises
irresistible. She knew, deep down,
that she was a monster, a predator
who walked among humans, playing
the role of the hunter while struggling
to contain the beast
within.

And she was afraid. Afraid of the
darkness, afraid of what she had
become, afraid of the monster
staring back at her from the mirror.
But most of all, she was afraid of
the emptiness, the hollowness that
threatened to consume her.

She knew she needed to find a way out. She had to choose between the life of a monster and the possibility of

redemption, however improbable it might seem. The weight of her past, the memories of her victims, they were a heavy burden to bear.

But she would keep fighting, keep searching for a way to break free from the chains of her own darkness. She would find a way, she had to. The alternative was too unbearable to contemplate, a life consumed by darkness, a soul forever stained by the blood of her victims.

It was a long and arduous path, but she knew she had to walk it. It was the only way she could hope to find peace, to find a shred of redemption, to find a way to stop the monster staring back at her from the mirror.

The Broken Mirror

The steam from the shower clung to the mirror, blurring her reflection into a hazy, almost ethereal figure. Elsa ran a hand through her damp hair, the movement a stark contrast to the stillness of her body. Her eyes, usually sharp and calculating, were clouded with a weary exhaustion that had settled deep in her bones.

She had walked the tightrope for so long, navigating the treacherous terrain of her own darkness, a world where the lines between right and wrong had become smudged, almost indistinguishable. The weight of her actions, the consequences of her choices, pressed down on her like an invisible burden, threatening to crush her beneath its crushing force.

The memory of the last confrontation, the final battle against the monstrous reflection of her own twisted psyche, replayed in her mind, the images as vivid and unsettling as the day they had occurred. The guttural scream that had ripped from her throat, the blood that had painted the city streets a macabre canvas of her desires, the chilling realization that she had become the very monster she had been tasked to hunt.

Elsa reached out a hand, tracing the outline of her reflection, the movement ghostlike in the steam-filled room. The reflection stared back at her, a hollow shell of the woman she had once been. The vibrant, defiant spark that had once burned bright in her eyes was now dimmed, replaced by a deep, unsettling emptiness. She had traded her innocence for a twisted sense of justice, her compassion for a cold, calculated acceptance of her own darkness.

The echoes of the past, the chilling memories of the victims she had hunted, of the lives she had taken, whispered in the back of her mind, a constant reminder of the horrors she had inflicted, the sins she had committed. The weight of guilt, a heavy cloak, wrapped itself around her, suffocating her with the knowledge of her own monstrosity.

There was no solace in the victories she had claimed, no satisfaction in the monsters she had subdued. Her triumphs felt hollow, tinged with a bitter aftertaste of self-loathing, a constant reminder of the chasm that had opened between her and the woman she had once aspired to be.

She had walked a path of darkness, each step pushing her further away from the light. The allure of her own twisted sense of justice had become a seductive siren song, luring her deeper and deeper into a world where morality was a distant memory, a mere whisper in the symphony of her own demons.

Elsa closed her eyes, the steam swirling around her, a shroud of her own making. She was trapped in a labyrinth of her own design, a world where the lines between hunter and hunted had blurred beyond recognition. The reflection in the broken mirror, a twisted caricature of the woman she had once been, stared back at her, a silent indictment of her choices.

The world outside her shower was a symphony of noise, the relentless pulse of the city a constant reminder of the life that went on, the lives she had touched, the lives she had shattered. It was a world she could no longer truly be a part of, a world she had condemned herself to observe from the fringes, forever haunted by the specter of her own past.

As she stood there, enveloped in the warmth of the steam

and the chilling reality of her own reflection, Elsa knew that there was no escaping the consequences of her actions. The broken mirror reflected not just the image of a woman, but the fractured pieces of her soul, a testament to the path she had chosen, the darkness she had embraced.

The weight of her decisions, the burden of her choices, was a heavy mantle she would carry for the rest of her life, a constant reminder of the price she had paid for her descent into darkness. The path ahead was uncertain, the future obscured by the swirling mist of her own regrets, the haunting whispers of her past. But Elsa knew one thing with a chilling certainty: there was no turning back. The darkness that had consumed her was a part of her now, woven into the fabric of her being, an inescapable truth reflected in the broken mirror of her soul.

The Search for Peace

The world had become a kaleidoscope of shattered reflections. The faces of her victims, their eyes filled with the echo of terror, haunted Elsa's sleep, a symphony of silent screams playing on repeat in her mind. She had traded the steel bars of a prison for the gilded cage of the CIA, a life where the darkness she craved was a twisted

form of
redemption, a perverse justice she
clung to.

Elsa was the hunter, the predator
stalking the shadows, but the shadows
were no longer solely those of others.
They were woven into her very being,
a tapestry of guilt and regret. Her
hands, once so adept at manipulating
the tools of death, now trembled with
the weight of her actions. She had
become a weapon, but the edge was
beginning to dull, a cruel irony she
couldn't escape.

The psychiatrist, Dr. Sinclair, was a
constant reminder of the fragile facade
she had built. His watchful gaze, his
probing questions, were like relentless
raindrops wearing down a stone. He

saw through her carefully crafted persona, the brittle shell that shielded her from the abyss within. His words, meant to dissect her soul, felt like a hammer on the anvil of her consciousness.

"Elsa, you are walking a tightrope, each step closer to the precipice. The darkness you fight, the demons you hunt, are also the demons within," he said, his voice a low thrum in the sterile silence of his office.

Elsa wanted to dismiss his words, to tell him that she
understood her path, that she had chosen this life, this
twisted redemption. But his words burrowed into her, stirring

a tempestuous storm within her. Was she truly fighting against the darkness, or was she simply embracing it, dancing with it?

She sought refuge in the adrenaline rush of the hunt, the thrill of the chase, the cold satisfaction of justice delivered. But the emptiness that followed, the hollowness that echoed in her heart, grew with each kill. The faces of her victims, the echoes of their screams, mingled with the faces of her past, a kaleidoscope of pain that threatened to consume her.

She tried to find solace in the solitude of her apartment, a fortress of steel and glass overlooking the city, a city that mirrored her own fractured psyche. But the silence, the solitude, was not her ally. It amplified the whispers, the accusations, the ghosts of her past.

One night, she stood at the window, her eyes reflecting the neon glow of the cityscape. The rain lashed against the glass, a rhythm that echoed the turmoil within. Below, the city pulsed with life, unaware of the darkness that lurked within its heart. The darkness she carried, the darkness she was destined to fight.

"Am I ever going to find peace?" she whispered, her voice lost in the relentless symphony of the city.

The answer was elusive, a ghost in the shadows, a question that echoed in the labyrinthine corridors of her mind. The search for peace, for atonement, had become her new obsession, a quest that was as dangerous as the hunts she had become accustomed to. She was a warrior, yes, but she was also a woman seeking redemption, a woman yearning for a peace she didn't know if she could ever find.

Elsa realized she was trapped in a vicious cycle. Each victory felt like a hollow victory, a temporary reprieve from the relentless torment. She had become the monster she was hunting, and she was beginning to wonder if she would ever be able to escape the cage she had built for herself.

The psychiatrist's words echoed in her mind, a constant reminder of the truth she couldn't deny. She had traded the security of a normal life for the dangerous freedom of a hunter, a freedom that was slowly becoming a prison of her own making. The world she had stepped into was a world of darkness, a world where the lines between good and evil were blurred, where the pursuit of justice often morphed into a twisted dance with the abyss.

Elsa found herself at a crossroads, a point where the path she had chosen threatened to unravel. The ghosts of her past, the weight of her sins, the emptiness that clung to her like a shroud, all demanded answers, all demanded a choice.

Would she continue to be the hunter, a weapon against the darkness that consumed her, or would she finally embrace the possibility of redemption, the possibility of a life beyond the shadows she had become so accustomed to?

The question hung in the air, a heavy silence that pressed down on her like a physical weight. Her reflection in the window seemed to mock her, a warped image of the woman she had become. The search for peace, for atonement, had become a desperate struggle, a fight against the darkness that threatened to consume her.

She knew that the path ahead was treacherous, filled with unforeseen dangers and internal battles that could shatter her to her core. Yet, she also knew that the only way to find peace, to find a semblance of redemption, was to face the darkness head-on. She had to stop running, stop hiding, and finally confront the truth that had haunted her for so long. It was a journey fraught with peril, a path that promised pain and uncertainty. But it was the only path towards the faint glimmer of hope that remained.

And so, Elsa Gardner, the woman who had embraced the darkness, the woman who had become the hunter, began her journey back from the abyss, her heart filled with a mixture of fear and determination. She would seek peace, she would find redemption, or she would be consumed by the shadows she had sought to control. It was a choice she had to make, a path she had to walk, a battle she had to fight. The fate of her soul hung in the balance.

The Shadow of the Past

The city lights blurred through the windshield, a kaleidoscope of neon and asphalt reflecting in Elsa's steely gaze. The hum of the engine was a constant companion, a hypnotic rhythm against the silence of her thoughts. Each passing street corner was a ghost, a phantom echo of her past. Her reflection in the rearview mirror, a pale, shadowed face, held the weight of a thousand whispered secrets.

She had done terrible things. The memories, sharp and vivid, sliced through her, a jagged reminder of the darkness she embraced. The goose, its life extinguished by her young hands, a chilling testament to her inherent nature. The college classmate, his lifeless eyes staring back at her, a silent accusation of her ruthlessness. Each victim, a phantom limb, tugging at the fabric of her soul, a constant reminder of the price she paid for her twisted sense of justice.

Her life had become a macabre dance, a relentless pursuit of the darkness within and without. The CIA had trained her, honed her skills, molded her into a weapon against the very evil she harbored. Yet, with each successful hunt, with each life extinguished by her hand, the guilt gnawed at her, a relentless serpent coiling around her heart.

The psychiatrist, Dr. Mason, a man who saw through her carefully crafted facade, was a constant source of both solace and torment. His probing questions, his unsettling insights, exposed the cracks in her carefully constructed world. He was a mirror reflecting her own fractured psyche, a reminder of the monstrous desires that lurked beneath the surface.

The shadow of her past loomed over her, an oppressive

weight that threatened to crush her. She was a hunter, a predator, but she was also the prey, a prisoner of her own darkness. She sought solace in the thrill of the hunt, the adrenaline rush of bringing a killer to justice, but it was a fleeting high, a temporary respite from the haunting memories that clung to her like a shroud.

The consequences of her choices were woven into the fabric of her existence. She had traded a life of normalcy for a life of shadows, a life where morality was a distant echo and redemption seemed like an impossible dream. Each kill, each victory, brought her closer to the precipice, a terrifying realization that the line between justice and self-destruction was razor-thin.

The world, once a canvas of hope and possibility, had become a bleak landscape, painted in shades of gray. She was a creature of

the night, a ghost in a world she could no longer recognize. But the darkness, the chilling truth that she was a serial killer, remained a constant, a shadow that
followed her every move, a haunting reminder of the price she paid for embracing the monster within.

The memory of her first kill, the chilling spectacle of a life snuffed out, still lingered in her mind. The victim's face, contorted in a mask of pain and terror, was a constant reminder of the fragility of life, the ease with which it could be shattered. It was a horrifying truth she couldn't escape, a twisted legacy she carried within.

The weight of those memories, heavy and oppressive, pressed down on her soul. She had sought to cleanse the world of evil, to punish the guilty, but in doing so, she had become a part of the very darkness she sought to eradicate. The guilt, the profound sense of regret, gnawed at her, a constant reminder of the terrible price she had paid.

She was no longer the young girl who had killed a goose in a fit of rage, a creature driven by primal impulses. She had evolved, matured, become a master of her craft, but the darkness remained, an indelible stain on her soul. The

memories, the whispers of her past, were a constant reminder that she was not a hero, not a savior, but a monster walking among men.

The psychiatrist's words, sharp and precise, echoed in her mind. He saw through her, understood the depths of her darkness. He was a constant threat, a reminder that her facade was crumbling, that her carefully constructed world was on the verge of collapse. He was a force she couldn't control, a voice that challenged her self-deception.

The city lights, once a symbol of hope and possibility, now seemed like a cruel mockery. They were a reminder of the life she had lost, the innocence

she had sacrificed. The world outside
her window was a swirling vortex of
chaos, a
reflection of the storm raging within
her.

The past, a relentless torrent of pain
and guilt, threatened to drown her.
The memories, sharp and vivid, were
a constant assault, a reminder of the
horrors she had inflicted. Yet, she
couldn't escape them, couldn't outrun
the darkness that clung to her like a
second skin.

She was a creature of duality, a
hunter and a hunted, a
predator and a prey. Her existence
was a tightrope walk, a precarious
dance between redemption and self-
destruction. The question was not

whether she would fall, but when, and what would be the cost.

The Uncertain Future

The aftermath of the final confrontation, the echoing silence of the city, bore the weight of her actions. Elsa stood in the chilling aftermath, the city lights blurring through the tears that streamed down her face. She had stopped him, the final predator, but the victory felt hollow, a bittersweet triumph.
The monster she had hunted, a reflection of her own

darkness, was finally vanquished. But the victory did not erase the stains of her past, the ghosts of those she had claimed for vengeance, the constant reminder of the darkness that lurked within her.

The world was a blurry tapestry of guilt and exhaustion. Her apartment, once a haven, now felt suffocating, the walls closing in on her with the weight of her secrets. Every corner whispered memories, reminding her of the choice she had made, the path she had chosen. She had become a weapon, an instrument of justice, but the lines had blurred. The hunter had become the hunted, the predator the prey.

She had known what she was becoming, had accepted the darkness within, yet the consequences of her actions gnawed at her soul. The psychiatrist, Dr. Evans, a man who had walked the tightrope with her, gazed at her with a weary understanding. He saw the weight of her burden, the
shattered reflection in her eyes, the fragile hope that clung to the precipice of despair.

"It's not about redemption, Elsa," he said, his voice a low, soothing tremor. "It's about acceptance. Accepting the darkness, the choices you have made, the person you have become."

She looked away, unable to face the truth he laid bare. "Acceptance is easy for you, Doctor," she hissed, her voice laced with resentment. "You haven't lived in the darkness, you haven't tasted the blood, felt the thrill of the hunt."

"No," he said, his gaze unwavering. "But I have seen the consequences. I have seen the monster you carry within, the one that threatens to consume you."

He reached out, placing a hand on her shoulder, his touch a gentle reminder of the humanity he saw within her. "It doesn't have to be this way, Elsa. There's still a chance to find a path, a different kind of justice, a different kind of life."

But the path he envisioned, the light he offered, seemed distant, a glimmer on the horizon that was obscured by the dense fog of her past. How could she, a woman who had embraced the darkness, find a way back to the light? The memories of her victims, the chilling truth of her choices, held her hostage. The city, her hunting ground, now seemed a menacing labyrinth, each corner whispering reminders of her descent.

Elsa's journey was far from over. The uncertainty of her future weighed heavily upon her. Could she truly find peace, could she find a way to atone for her actions, or was the darkness she had embraced destined to consume her? The questions, like shadowy specters, haunted her waking hours and tormented her dreams.

She spent her days in the confines of her apartment, a prison of her own making. The city, once a playground for her twisted sense of justice, now seemed a menacing labyrinth, each corner whispering reminders of her descent. The faces of her victims, the whispers of their silenced screams, haunted her dreams.

Dr. Evans, her constant observer, continued to monitor her progress, a beacon in the storm. He saw the vulnerability beneath her hardened exterior, the fear that lurked in her eyes, the yearning for a path back from the darkness. He had dedicated himself to helping her, to guiding her towards a semblance of peace, a path to redemption.

He had warned her of the dangers of the path she had chosen, the inevitable consequences of her actions. But she had been resolute, driven by a twisted sense of justice, a desire to punish those who had inflicted pain upon others.

Now, she was left with the chilling realization that her actions had been a double-edged sword, a dance with a darkness that threatened to consume her entirely.

Elsa's journey had been a descent into the abyss, a relentless chase for justice that had taken its toll. She had lost a part of herself, a part that was irrevocably stained by the blood of her victims, the echoes of their screams forever etched in her memory. The guilt, like a relentless tide, threatened to engulf her, pulling her deeper into the depths of despair.

But amidst the darkness, a small flicker of hope remained.
Dr. Evans, with his unwavering belief in her capacity for change, offered a lifeline, a path back from the brink. He saw the remnants of the woman she once was, the woman who had dreamt of a world free from injustice,

a world where the darkness was banished and the light shone brightly.

The road ahead was long and arduous. Elsa had to confront the demons she had unleashed, the horrors she had inflicted, and the darkness that had taken root within her. The journey to redemption, if it existed, would be a battle fought within the confines of her own tormented mind.

Yet, in the face of the overwhelming darkness, Elsa clung to

the hope that Dr. Evans had ignited within her. She had been a monster, a predator, but the faint whispers of redemption, though barely audible, remained. The future, a canvas painted in the hues of darkness and uncertainty, held the potential for a new beginning. But only if Elsa could summon the courage to embrace the path towards healing, towards a future where the monster within could be subdued, where the darkness could be replaced by the flicker of a hope.

The Whispers of Redemption

The city's relentless rain had become a backdrop to Elsa's life, mirroring the relentless storm brewing inside her. The weight of her past, the victims she'd claimed, the darkness she'd embraced - all of it pressed against her like a

suffocating blanket. Her apartment felt like a cage, the walls closing in on her, each breath a reminder of the twisted path she'd chosen. She'd spent years hunting down the shadows that lurked in the city, battling her own inner demons, a silent dance with the abyss. But now, a flicker of something else was stirring within her - a flicker of hope.

The case, her latest prey - a serial killer known as the 'Night Weaver' - had been particularly harrowing. His methods were a brutal symphony of torture and death, echoing the darkest corners of Elsa's own mind. But it was during a particularly brutal interrogation that she'd stumbled upon a clue, a thread leading to a different, unsettling truth. The Night Weaver's victims, she realized, were not random. They were connected to Elsa, to her past, a cruel mirror reflecting her own deepest secrets.

It was a revelation that had shaken her to her core. This wasn't just another hunt; it was a twisted reflection of her own journey. The fear that had been her constant companion transformed into something else, something primal,
something that whispered of a forgotten truth, a truth she'd buried deep within her psyche, fearing the light it might cast on her own

darkness.

She'd sought refuge in the familiar comfort of her therapist's office, the sterile white walls offering no solace. Dr. Sinclair, a man who'd witnessed her descent into the abyss, listened

patiently, his eyes a deep, unwavering blue, reflecting the storm raging within her.

"It's like...like I'm looking into a mirror, but the reflection is warped, twisted," Elsa confessed, her voice barely a whisper.
"I'm seeing myself in him, in the way he kills, the way he chooses

his victims..."

Dr. Sinclair, his face a mask of impassive calm, leaned back in his chair, a single, silver pen spinning between his fingers.
"And how does that make you feel, Elsa?" he asked, his voice a soothing balm in the chaos within her.

"It makes me feel..." Elsa struggled to find the words, the sensation a tangled knot in her stomach. "It makes me feel like I'm trapped, Dr. Sinclair. Like I'm in this endless cycle, hunting down these people, only to realize they are a part of me, a part of what I've always been afraid to confront."

"And what are you afraid to confront, Elsa?" he pressed gently.

"The truth, Dr. Sinclair. The truth about the darkness inside me, the truth about why I chose this path."

She wasn't afraid of the killing, not anymore. It was a part of her, an extension of the darkness that lived inside her, a darkness she embraced. But there was a deeper fear, a fear that she couldn't name, a fear that gnawed at the edges of her sanity, a fear of understanding the truth behind the monster she had become.

"Perhaps," Dr. Sinclair said slowly, his voice a silken thread weaving through the storm inside her. "Perhaps this is your chance to finally face that truth, Elsa. To confront the

demons you've been running from, to understand the roots of your darkness. To finally find a way to break free."

His words, though offered with the utmost care, struck her like a thunderbolt. He was right. Perhaps this twisted

reflection in the Night Weaver, this chilling echo of her past, was the key to unlocking the chains that bound her to the darkness. It was a chance to confront the monsters she'd buried, to break free from the cycle of violence that consumed her.

The possibility, however terrifying, sparked a flicker of hope within her. A hope that, despite the abyss that consumed her, a glimmer of redemption, a flicker of light, might still exist. She wasn't ready to let go of the power she'd embraced, the thrill of the hunt, the intoxicating rush of her own darkness. But perhaps, just perhaps, there was a different path, a path that led not to oblivion, but to a semblance of peace.

The storm raged on within her, but for the first time, she felt a sliver of calm amidst the chaos. She could feel the shackles of her past loosen, the truth whispering to her, promising a path towards something more than just survival. It was a path she'd feared, a path she'd resisted, but now, she felt a strange pull towards it, a pull towards the light that might just illuminate the darkness within her.

It was a long shot, a risky gamble, but for the first time in a very long time, Elsa felt a flicker of hope, a flicker of possibility, a whisper of redemption. The whispers were faint, barely audible, but they were there, a beacon in the storm, beckoning her towards a future she'd never dared to dream of.

The Final Choice

The air hung heavy in the sterile room, a suffocating blanket of silence broken only by the rhythmic ticking of the clock on the wall. Elsa sat across from Dr. Thorne, her usual cool detachment replaced by a raw, unfiltered vulnerability that made her feel exposed.

"You're not a monster, Elsa," Dr. Thorne said, his voice a soothing balm against the storm brewing inside her. "You're a woman with a past that has shaped you, a past that has twisted your perception of right and wrong."

His words were a lifeline in the sea of uncertainty that had become her reality. For years, she had clung to the illusion of control, of being the

hunter, the one who dealt justice to those who deserved it. But the more she delved into the dark recesses of her own psyche, the more the line between
justice and vengeance blurred.

"But I am capable of such things," Elsa whispered, her voice barely audible above the hum of the air conditioner. The chilling truth of her actions, the weight of each life she had taken, pressed down on her like an unbearable burden.

"We all have the capacity for darkness, Elsa," Dr. Thorne said, his gaze unwavering. "The difference lies in our choices. You can choose to remain on this path, consumed by your demons, or you can choose to fight for something different, something better."

The choice hung heavy in the air, a gaping chasm separating the world she knew from the one she longed for. She had spent years embracing her darkness, using it as a shield, a

weapon against a world that had wronged her. But now, with a clarity she had never known before, she saw the futility of it all.

The faces of her victims flickered in her mind, a chilling tableau of guilt and regret. The goose, its lifeless body sprawled on the grass, the innocent college classmate whose life had been brutally extinguished, the predator she had lured to his demise. Each face a stark reminder of the darkness she had embraced, the darkness that now threatened to consume her.

A single tear traced a path down her cheek, a silent acknowledgment of the pain she had inflicted, the lives she had taken. She closed her eyes, the echoes of her past actions reverberating in the chamber of her soul.

"I've killed," she whispered, the words laden with a weight that pressed down on her chest. "I've destroyed. I've taken lives."

"Yes, you have," Dr. Thorne said, his voice gentle but firm. "But you can also choose to create. To heal. To make
amends."

His words were like a spark in the darkness, igniting a
flickering ember of hope in her heart. She had spent so long clinging to the illusion of control, of being the hunter, the one who dealt justice. But the truth was, she was trapped in a cycle of violence, a self-perpetuating darkness that
threatened to consume her entirely.

The choice, as always, was hers.

She could continue on this path, a solitary wolf, forever haunted by the ghosts of her past. Or she could reach out, embrace the possibility of redemption, and try to forge a new

path.

The clock ticked relentlessly, each second a beat of her own inner drum, a rhythm that dictated the tempo of her life. She knew she couldn't escape her past, the darkness that had become an inextricable part of her being. But she could choose to move forward, to fight for something different, something better.

Elsa opened her eyes, the reflection of the room's cold fluorescent lights mirroring the turmoil within her. But within that chaos, a flicker of hope, a whisper of redemption.

"I want to try," she said, her voice raspy, the words a testament to the internal struggle raging within her. "I want to try to be different."

Dr. Thorne nodded, a small smile playing on his lips. "Then you will," he said, his voice filled with a gentle encouragement that resonated within her. "You will find a way."

The weight of the world, the burden of her past, seemed to lift slightly, replaced by a glimmer of hope, a sense of possibility. It wouldn't be easy. The path to redemption, if it existed, was a treacherous one, fraught with obstacles and dangers.

But for the first time in a long time, Elsa felt a flicker of something else, something she had almost forgotten existed: Hope. The hope for a future where she could be more than the darkness that consumed her. The hope for a future where she could choose to be different.

As she left the sterile confines of Dr. Thorne's office, Elsa knew the journey ahead would be arduous. The scars of her past, the indelible marks of her darkness, would always be a

part of her. But now, she carried something else within her, something that had been dormant for so long: The will to fight for a future where she could choose to be better, to choose to be different.
The final dance had just begun.

The Turning Tide

The rain hammered against the window, a relentless rhythm mirroring the storm raging within Elsa. Her apartment, usually a sanctuary of controlled chaos, felt suffocating. The air hung heavy with the scent of stale coffee and the cloying sweetness of her own fear. She hadn't slept in days, the constant hum of her inner turmoil a symphony of dread.

The psychiatrist, Dr. Lawson, had become her constant companion, his watchful gaze a constant reminder of her precarious existence. He saw through her carefully constructed façade, recognizing the monster she desperately tried to hide. His analysis was chillingly accurate, each session a dissection of her twisted psyche, a relentless exploration of the darkness that festered within.

"You're not a monster, Elsa," he'd
said, his voice calm yet piercing.
"You're a human being grappling
with a profound darkness."

But his words offered no solace. She
knew he was right. But it was a truth
that chilled her to the bone, a truth she
fought against with every fiber of her
being. She wasn't a monster.
Not in the sense of a mindless
beast, driven solely by instinct. No,
her darkness was something more
complex, a tapestry woven from the
threads of pain, betrayal, and a
thirst for vengeance that consumed
her.

The CIA had offered her a lifeline, a
chance to channel her darkness, to
become a weapon against the very

evil that haunted her. But with each kill, each successful mission, the weight of her actions pressed down on her, a crushing

burden she couldn't escape. Her life had become a twisted

dance, a waltz with death, a constant struggle to maintain control over the predator that lurked beneath the surface.

The faces of her victims, the echoes of their screams, haunted her every waking moment. Each life taken was a stain on her soul, a testament to the depths of her own depravity. She could rationalize it, convince herself it was justice, but the truth was undeniable. She was a killer, and the line between hero and villain had long since blurred.

Tonight, she stood at a crossroads, her internal struggle reaching a fever pitch. She felt a shift within, a tremor of something different, something that whispered of a different path.

It started with a dream, a vivid hallucination that had seeped into her waking hours, a memory so potent it had shaken her to her core. A childhood memory, long buried beneath layers of trauma and self-defense, but now resurfacing with a raw, undeniable force.

The memory of her father, the man who had shattered her world, the source of her pain and her rage. The memory of his violence, the chilling touch of his hand, the terror that had consumed her, leaving a gaping wound that had never truly healed.

And then, a voice, a soft whisper, a whisper of hope. A voice that resonated from the deepest recesses of her soul, a voice that dared to question the narrative of her life, the narrative of her darkness.

It spoke of a different truth, a truth that was buried beneath the layers of her rage and her pain. A truth that whispered of forgiveness, of redemption, of a path that led away from the abyss.

The whispers grew stronger,
pushing against the darkness that
had consumed her for so long. They
spoke of a future where she wasn't a
weapon, where she wasn't a
predator, where she wasn't a
prisoner of her own demons.

Elsa felt her resolve crumble, her
carefully constructed walls of self-
defense dissolving in the face of this
new truth. The whispers were a siren
song, beckoning her towards a
different shore, a shore where she
could finally find peace, where she

could finally be free.

But it was a path fraught with peril, a path that demanded she confront her past, her demons, her darkest self. It was a path that required her to let go of the pain, the anger, the vengeance that had defined her for so long.

It was a path that demanded she choose redemption, a path that demanded she choose to live.

The storm within Elsa raged on, but beneath the tempest, a faint flicker of hope began to ignite. A glimmer of
possibility, a promise of something different.

The turning tide was upon her, and she knew that the choice she made now would shape the rest of her destiny.

The Unveiling of Truth

The air hung thick with anticipation, heavy with the weight of years of secrets and lies. Elsa stood in the center of the cavernous warehouse, a single spotlight illuminating her like a predator poised to strike. She was surrounded by men in suits, their faces a mask of indifference as they observed her, their eyes cold and calculating. In the back, a small group of reporters buzzed with anticipation, their cameras trained on her.

This was it. The final act.

Elsa knew what they were waiting for, what they needed to see. They had gathered here to hear her confession, to
witness the unraveling of the woman they had known as Elsa Gardner, the CIA's weapon against the darkness. But there was more to it than that. This wasn't just a confession; it was a reckoning, a confrontation with the truth that had haunted her since childhood.

She looked at them, her eyes cold and calculating, a flicker of defiance in their depths. She had played the game, danced to their tune, but now, the music had changed. The truth was no longer a tool to be wielded, a weapon to be used against others. It was her truth, and it would be her weapon.

"I killed them," she said, her voice a low, dangerous murmur, echoing through the warehouse. "Every single one. The college student, the man who assaulted my roommate, the men who took my life and my future."

The room went silent, a pin drop audible in the oppressive quiet. Her words were a bomb, exploding in the air,

shattering the facade of control
that had been carefully
constructed around her.

"But it wasn't about justice," she
continued, her voice
gaining strength. "It wasn't about
making the world a better place. It
was about something else. Something
much darker."

A collective gasp rippled through the
audience. They leaned forward, their
faces a mixture of shock and morbid
fascination. They had known she was
dangerous, but this –this was
something else. This was a peek

into the abyss.

"I'm not a hero," she continued, her voice cold and unflinching. "I'm not a savior. I'm a monster. I'm a predator. And I've been hunting for a long time."

Elsa's confession was not a plea for forgiveness, it was a declaration of war. She was not begging for their understanding, she was demanding their attention. She had played their game, danced to their tune, but now, the music had changed.

She spoke of her childhood, a tapestry of pain and trauma. She spoke of the day her father was killed in a senseless act of violence, a day that forever altered the course of her life.

"I was seven years old," she said, her voice raspy with emotion. "I watched as a man shot my father, a man who had done nothing to deserve it. He was a stranger, a random target in a city filled with violence. But to me, he was the embodiment of evil, the personification of the pain that had taken my father from me."

Her voice dropped to a whisper. "And that day, something inside me broke. Something inside me shifted. I felt a rage, a hatred, a desire for retribution that was primal, instinctive. I wanted to make him pay."

She described the obsession that consumed her, the longing for vengeance that grew with each passing year. It wasn't about right or wrong, it was about instinct, about survival. It was about finding a way to control the darkness that threatened to consume her.

She told them about her first kill, about the satisfaction that followed, the thrill of the hunt, the sense of power. It was a dark pleasure, a twisted sense of justice, a way to make sense of the chaos. But it wasn't enough.

She spoke of her years at college, her carefully constructed facade, the mask she wore to hide the monster within. It was a game she played, a performance she gave, but the darkness inside her never truly left.

"I was always looking for the next target," she admitted. "I was always searching for a way to make sense of the world. I wanted to believe that there was a reason for the pain, that there was a purpose to the chaos. But I was lost."

She described the day she was caught, the moment she was forced to confront the reality of her actions. She was a
monster, a predator, and she was

caught in a web of her own creation.

"But it was a moment of clarity," she said, her voice steady.
"It was a moment of truth. I knew that I couldn't keep
running, that I couldn't keep hiding. I knew that I had to face the darkness inside me."

Elsa looked at the room, her eyes reflecting the darkness of the warehouse. She had confessed to her crimes, she had revealed the truth of her being, but she was not seeking redemption. She was seeking understanding.

She knew that they would judge her, that they would fear her. She was a monster, after all. But she was also a product of a world filled with darkness. She was a reflection of the pain and the chaos that surrounded her.

"I'm not asking for your forgiveness," she said, her voice firm. "I'm not asking for your understanding. But I am
asking you to see me. See me for what I am. See me for what you made me."

She knew that her confession would change nothing. It was not a plea for mercy, it was a declaration of war. She was a monster, and she would continue to hunt, to stalk, to kill. But now, she would do it with a sense of

purpose, with a
knowledge of her own darkness.

The room was silent, the reporters
still, their cameras
flashing like lightning. The world
outside the warehouse had been
shattered, the illusion of control
broken. But Elsa was still standing,
her gaze unwavering. She was a
monster, but she was also a woman
who had found her truth, and she
would face the darkness head-on.

Elsa's confession was not a plea for
forgiveness, it was a declaration of
war. She was not begging for their
understanding, she was demanding
their attention. She had played their
game, danced to their tune, but now,

the music had changed.

This was not the end, it was just the beginning.

The truth had been unveiled, and
the darkness had been embraced.
But Elsa's journey was far from
over.

The Last Dance

The air hung heavy with the scent of
jasmine and decay, a strange perfume
that clung to the humid night like a
second skin. Elsa stood at the
precipice of the rooftop, the city

sprawled beneath her like a canvas of shadows and flickering neon. The wind whipped her hair around her face, carrying with it the distant sirens of a world she had abandoned long ago.

She had come to the rooftop, as she had done so many times before, to breathe. To feel the sting of the wind against her skin, the cold metal of the railing against her calloused palms. It was her sanctuary, a place where she could shed the mask of the hunter and confront the beast that resided within.

But tonight, the beast felt different. The familiar thrum of violence pulsed beneath her skin, not with the manic energy of a predator on the hunt, but with the dull ache of a creature facing its final reckoning.

The psychiatrist, Dr. William Carter, had been right. The darkness had been festering, spreading like a malignant tumor through her soul. The killings, once fueled by a twisted sense of justice, had become a means to feed the insatiable hunger within. Each life she took, each twisted game she played, left a stain on her conscience, a reminder of the monster she had become.

She closed her eyes, the memories flooding back in a relentless tide. The goose, its lifeless eyes staring back at her, the fear and innocence of her first victim, the cold steel of the knife sinking into flesh.

The faces, the names, the stories– they all echoed in the silent chambers of her mind, a
chorus of ghosts she could never outrun.

She had been a soldier in the war against darkness, but the battle had turned her into the very thing she hunted. She had become the monster, the predator, the executioner. And with each kill, the monster had grown, until it had consumed her entire being.

"I am the darkness," she whispered, her voice lost to the howling wind. "I am the hunter, and the hunted."

Tonight, the whispers of doubt were louder than ever. She was a chess piece in a game she didn't understand, a pawn in a grand scheme orchestrated by forces she couldn't comprehend. The CIA, her supposed salvation, had become her prison, a cage built of twisted morals and cold, calculated ambition. She was a weapon, a tool for a system that offered no redemption.

Dr. Carter had tried to warn her, to pull her back from the abyss, but his words had fallen on deaf ears. She had dismissed him as a mere observer, a psychiatrist playing a game of psychology with a damaged soul. But in the shadows of her own darkness, she had begun to see the truth in his words. She was unraveling, her carefully crafted façade crumbling under the weight of her own sins.

She could feel the psychiatrist's presence, his watchful gaze piercing through the darkness. He was a ghost in the
shadows, a constant reminder of the sanity she was losing, the humanity she was abandoning. He had tried to show her the path to redemption, but she had chosen a different road, a road paved with blood and despair.

Tonight, she stood at the crossroads, forced to confront the truth of her own existence. She was a broken vessel, a walking contradiction, a predator seeking redemption. She had become the very thing she was fighting against.

And in the depths of her despair, she found a glimmer of hope. Not the false hope of a system that worshipped power and exploited darkness, but the hope of a soul seeking
redemption, a creature yearning to break free from the chains of its own creation.

Her journey was far from over, but she had reached a turning point. The last dance had begun, a dance with her own

demons, a dance with fate. The music was a symphony of guilt and despair, but in the midst of the chaos, a melody of hope whispered through the air. It was a whisper, a fragile melody, but it was enough. Enough to pull her back from the brink, enough to show her a way forward.

Elsa closed her eyes, taking a deep breath. The night wind carried the scent of jasmine and decay, but beneath the darkness, she could sense the faintest glimmer of a new dawn. She had come to the rooftop to confront her demons, but she had also come to find herself. And as the city lights shimmered beneath her, she knew that the last dance had just begun.

Appendix

This appendix contains a collection
of supplementary
materials related to the story,
offering additional insight into the
world of Elsa Gardner and the
complexities of her
journey.

Elsa's Journal Entries:

A selection of personal journal
entries, penned by Elsa, reveal her
innermost thoughts, fears, and
justifications for her actions.

The CIA's Serial Killer
Database:

A glimpse into the classified

database of the CIA,
showcasing profiles of notorious
serial killers and their twisted
methods.

The Psychiatrist's Notes:
A compilation of the
psychiatrist's clinical notes,
documenting his observations and
insights into Elsa's psyche.

Glossary

This glossary defines key terms and
concepts relevant to the story:

Psychopathy:
A personality disorder characterized

by a lack of empathy, remorse, and guilt, often accompanied by manipulative behaviors.

Antisocial Personality Disorder:
A personality disorder characterized by a disregard for social norms, a lack of empathy, and a history of criminal behavior.

Modus Operandi (MO):
The method or pattern of operation used by a criminal, particularly in the context of serial crimes.

Macabre:
Gruesome, disturbing, and morbid.

Printed in Great Britain
by Amazon